FACT

The Un...

SECRET

Behind the Story

In 1912, the collector Wilfred Voynich discovered a selection of ancient books hidden in a chest in Mondragone Castle, Italy. Among the texts was a manuscript written entirely in code. It became known as the Voynich Manuscript.

For a century, academics tried to break the code. But not a single word or phrase in the 245 pages of the Voynich Manuscript has been read.

In 1944 a group of code-breakers working for the US government formed a Study Group to try and decipher the text. They failed. Between 1962 and 1963 a second Study Group was formed. Eventually Americans joined with British code-breakers based at Bletchley Park Mansion. They failed.

In 1969 the manuscript was donated to Yale University and registered simply as 'MS 408'. It is kept hidden from general view in the Beinecke Rare Book and Manuscript Library. Since that day, the secret code has remained unbroken.

UNTIL NOW ...

Also by H. L. Dennis

SECRET BREAKERS

SECRET BREAKERS

TOWER OF THE WINDS

H. L. Dennis

Illustrations by Meggie Dennis

Hodder
Children's
Books

A division of Hachette Children's Books

For John and Tusia Werner
and inspirational teachers everywhere.

And in memory of
Rosemary Ingham,
teacher, writer and friend.

Ignorance, the root and the stem of every evil.

Plato

I cannot live without books.

Thomas Jefferson

Angel of Death

Brodie Bray was about to die.

She was aware of every fibre of her body, every pulse of her heart, every tightening of her muscles. Her senses were heightened. Time slowed down. She knew she'd never have the answers she'd been looking for.

She didn't call out or struggle. Hunter Jenkins wasn't going to be able to save her this time. Hunter and the rest of her friends in Team Veritas were about to die as well.

The noise warning of approaching death began as a low rumble. A gentle thunder murmuring through the dark.

The ground trembled. Then a light, round and brilliant, rose to engulf the room. A whining scream pierced the air. Brodie pulled her arms up to her head. But the light burned through her fingers and the noise sliced at her ears.

A huge black shape rose in the sky outside the windows of Bletchley Park Mansion, stretching on darkened wings. And the panes shuddered in the casings. Then they shattered. Shards of glass exploded across the room. The wooden supports shook for a moment then collapsed. A blast of icy air surged into the room, lifting pages and papers in a swirling churn of destruction. And the sound of the mechanical screeching throbbed in Brodie's ears as her nostrils filled with the stench of burning rubber and petrol.

Brodie waited for the darkness.

It didn't come.

Instead, light blazed across the ceiling above her as the screeching faltered, spluttered and then died.

Brodie opened her eyes. A circle of light slid down the wall and pooled across the floor.

Lying on its side, with its wheels still spinning in the air and its headlight burning, was a motorbike, and staggering to stand beside it, dressed head to toe in leather, was its rider.

It was odd how an angel of death transforming into a leather-clad biker didn't at once make Brodie feel safer. The biker brought destruction. He'd broken into the team's home and he reached now for a long, thin black box and held it up in the air.

He was reaching for a gun. He'd broken into Bletchley to kill them. Sent by Level Five to stop them breaking the code of the ancient manuscript they'd worked so hard to understand. Brodie knew she should kneel down and surrender but she stood perfectly still.

If he took her away, she wouldn't give up the battle to read what the government had banned them from trying to read. She'd find a way to reach the others – re-form the team. They'd tried too hard for too long to give up easily. The leather-clad biker could take away her freedom but he'd never take away her desire to find the truth.

The biker clutched the box against him, but didn't open it. Instead, he shook the shards of glass from his shoulders and put the box on the ground. Then he reached up and removed his helmet.

Brodie tried, then, to make sense of what she saw.

The biker was a woman. Long wavy hair tumbled untidily across her shoulders. She was twenty at the oldest, her face freckled and blushing. She staggered awkwardly then steadied herself before speaking. 'Really sorry about that, everyone. I'm new to this biking game and I can't begin to apologise enough for the mess I've made.'

'Kitty? Kitty McCloud?'

Sheldon was speaking. He'd got up from his sprawling position on the floor and was moving across the room, through the debris and the chaos, his hair dusted with brick dust, his forehead furrowed like he was peering through fog trying to see the road ahead.

The woman smiled.

'You know her?' Brodie exclaimed, her voice several octaves higher than usual.

'Yep, from The Plough.' The Plough was the pub Sheldon had lived in with his mother before Team Veritas had made a visit and decided with his musical skills and knowledge he'd make a great addition to the group. 'Kitty was a barmaid there. One of the few people who stood up to my mum.' He made his way across the room and opened his arms to give the biker an enthusiastic hug. Kitty McCloud responded eagerly. 'How on earth did you find us?' Sheldon asked her. 'No one knew we were here.'

'The Christmas turkey,' explained Kitty, shaking a new rain of glass fragments from her shoulders. 'Your mum had it sent to PO Box London 111. I did some digging and found that in the Second World War, PO Box 111 was here. So I put two and two together and here I am.'

'Here you are indeed,' said Mr Smithies, the leader of the team. He wiped a cloud of dust from his jacket as he spoke. 'But I presume the gates to the mansion were locked. This was, we believed, a fairly secure environment.'

Kitty's cheeks coloured. 'Yep, that's where it started to go wrong really. With the bike, I mean. Like I say, I haven't been riding long, but messing about at home across the hills, I learnt to jump the thing.'

'Oh, please.' Sicknote Ingham had been cowering in the corner, but the mention of jumping a motorbike caused him to swoon into a nearby chair and dab at his face with a large spotted handkerchief.

'I managed to jump the gate no problem,' Kitty rushed on, 'but I think I've jammed the throttle. I lost control on the driveway trying to avoid that crazy water feature on the edge of the lake and, well . . .' Her voice tailed away. 'Nice place you've got here, though,' she said more cheerfully. 'Sort of retro.'

'It was,' moaned Sicknote.

'Don't worry,' said Tusia. 'Bikes tend to cause trouble round here.'

Brodie thought back to the first time she'd met Hunter outside the doors to the mansion and how she'd crashed into him while he'd been riding a unicycle. The unicycle hadn't come off well. It had

5

taken Friedman ages working on it in secret to mend. Brodie's stomach tightened a little at the thought of Friedman. He used to be one of the adult members of the team, perhaps the one she'd worked most closely with. He'd turned out to be a traitor and a deceiver and towards the end of the summer she'd discovered he was with her mother when she died. No one had known that before.

Friedman wasn't part of the team any more. Brodie was pretty sure he'd changed sides and was working for Level Five now the truth about her mum was out.

'It was the bike that did it,' Kitty was saying. 'Not my bike. But Elgar's.'

It was Sheldon's turn to look awkward now. After meeting Sheldon at a museum, the team had originally set off back to Bletchley Park Mansion without him. But Sheldon had caught them up. On a stolen bike. One which had once belonged to the composer Elgar. Complicated research helped the team find out the famous composer was linked to the unreadable manuscript and Sheldon, knowing lots about Elgar, helped them discover more.

'The Elgar Museum noticed the bike was missing, then?' said Sheldon uncomfortably.

'Course they did,' said Kitty. 'It was all over the

local news and the papers. Brought lots of other visitors to the museum, which was good for a while.'

'A while?'

Kitty's face darkened. 'A woman arrived, just before Christmas. Wanted to know if anything else had been taken from the museum.'

It wasn't only Elgar's bike the team had added to their collection at Bletchley. There was a map book and a letter written to Elgar from his musical publisher Jaeger. 'People know we've taken the map and letter?' Brodie asked nervously.

'Evie knew.'

Evie was a guide at the museum.

Kitty's face formed a troubled frown. 'Once Evie realised the bike was gone, she carried out a total inventory of the place.'

'And she told the visitor what we took?' pressed Smithies.

Kitty nodded.

'So why'd that bring you here?' Sheldon steered Kitty towards an undamaged chair so she could answer. She was looking a little peaky.

'Evie's gone missing.'

Now Sheldon looked in need of a chair. Evie was a great fan of Sheldon's and encouraged him to play the piano in the museum even though his mother thought his love of music was a waste of time. 'What do you mean, gone missing?'

'She's vanished,' said Kitty. 'Stopped coming into the Plough for her medium sherry each night after the museum closed. So I did some asking around. Found she wasn't turning up at the museum at all. She wasn't at home. People rang and she just didn't return their calls.'

'What did her family say?' asked Tusia.

'Evie's got none. The Elgar Museum was everything. That's why she was so keen to explain to the visitor what was taken. And then, after that, she disappeared.' An uncomfortable silence hung across the room. 'I guessed that somehow you leaving and Evie vanishing must be connected and so eventually I asked your mum where you'd gone. She said you'd been chosen to be part of this special team and she wasn't sure really where it was.'

'Wasn't like she was going to pay a visit anytime, was it?' said Sheldon, trying to sound less hurt than he obviously was.

'So I decided I had to find you,' Kitty continued. 'Try and work out what happened.'

'I know exactly what's happened,' moaned Smithies. 'Kerrith.' He spat the word as if it burnt in his mouth.

'This isn't good,' mumbled Sicknote. 'What about

the others we've spoken to when we've been investigating the code? There's that woman from the Highgate Literary and Scientific Institution in London? Mr Willer in Chepstow?'

'D'you think Kerrith and her team have got on to them as well?' asked Tandi, whose face had the same look of anger she always wore if one of the team she helped look after seemed to be in danger.

Smithies surveyed the devastation of the room. 'This could be really bad.'

Kitty shuffled her feet, scraping against the broken glass. 'Look, I didn't mean to do all this,' she said, gesturing once more to the chaos she'd made. 'I've no idea what you're up to here. I just guessed it was important. And I guessed, if you needed a letter from Jaeger to Elgar to help you do whatever you were doing, well then – you might need this.'

She reached down and lifted the long, thin black box Brodie had been so sure held a gun and rested it on her knees before clicking the lid open.

'My flute,' yelped Sheldon, lurching forward. 'Oh, you total star,' he added, reaching for the instrument as she took it from its bed of soft blue velvet.

'And these . . .' said Kitty, drawing out a roll of papers from inside the first section of the silver instrument. 'More letters written between Elgar and

9

Jaeger. Evie told me they were important. She was kind of nervy after that visitor came and she wanted to make sure everything was in order. The letters weren't on show in the museum, or even in Elgar's desk where the one you found was kept.'

Brodie squirmed a little at the memory of how they'd searched the desk while Sheldon played the piano in the room next door to distract the other visitors.

'When the woman came asking Evie questions, Evie told me about this secret supply of letters. She said loads of the letters between Elgar and Jaeger were burnt in a house fire in World War One, but these survived. She wanted me to keep them in the safe at the Plough so there was no chance of them being stolen. After she went missing, I began to worry about whether I should tell anyone I had them.' She looked across the room at Sheldon. 'Evie thought the world of you. The grandson she never had. Family, really. That's why I came.'

Brodie took the letters and they passed them round. There were no obvious codes to see. No cipher wheels or lumps and bumps to decipher. No letters written darker than any others. Brodie guessed they were just like the other letters they'd rejected from the desk back at the museum. Not everything contained a code.

Kitty smiled awkwardly as she took them back.

'You did a good thing,' Smithies said, and even amid the cold and the chaos, Brodie was almost sure he was right.

'I say we have to trust her.' Tandi Tandari sounded very sure.

Tandi had once worked as Smithies' secretary before the old man had set up Team Veritas and Tandi had insisted she came with him. She'd explained to Brodie she'd been obsessed with the unreadable manuscript MS 408 for years and would stop at nothing to help Smithies build a team to solve it. She was a determined woman and she seemed determined now, her expression set hard, her black eyes blazing.

The team had allowed Kitty to spend the night at Bletchley in one of the rooms in the mansion, and while a gang of contractors came to repair the damage to the windows of the ballroom, the team met in Hut 11 to decide what they should do with her.

'I'm not sure,' said Smithies. 'She's an outsider.'

'We were all outsiders once,' said Sheldon awkwardly.

'Yes, but you were all invited. Because of the skills you had. Your musical skills. Brodie's story skills, Tusia's shape and space awareness and Hunter's maths. Anything this Kitty knows about Elgar can't be as good as what you already know.'

11

Sheldon puffed out his chest a little.

'Well, maybe we need her sense of adventure,' said Tandi. 'You've got to admit she's a risk taker.'

'She's a health and safety disaster,' snapped Sicknote. 'I think this team's taken enough risks letting two senior citizens like me and Mr Bray be involved.'

It was true, with Granddad's dodgy leg and Sicknote's many ailments the team certainly had enough health issues to contend with without adding the risk of dangerous driving.

'But she's brought us a lead,' went on Tandi. 'She's worked out we may be on to something important and she's taken a risk to bring it here. Don't we owe it to her to explain?'

Fabyan, the American billionaire who'd made sure they had the money needed to work on cracking the code of MS 408, coughed gently into his fist. 'Isn't the question really whether we want to add anyone else to the team?'

'Well, yes. There's that too. And so,' Tandi scanned the room looking for encouragement to go on, 'I've been thinking.'

'Go on,' said Smithies.

'Kitty told us Evie's missing. That got me wondering if other people we've asked about the code were safe. I rang the Highgate Institution this morning.'

'And?'

'They told me Miss Longman hadn't been in to volunteer there for a while.'

There was a thickening of the air.

'The man on the phone said it was odd because they knew how much Miss Longman loved what she did there. He hadn't seen her for ages though.'

'This isn't good,' blurted Tusia. 'There's no way the old dear would have left.'

'And he told me,' continued Tandi, 'some woman had been in to pick up a printout of a letter we asked for and never collected.'

'The death-bed letter written by Sir Francis Bacon!' groaned Hunter. 'We never went back for the printout. Miss Longman gave us a copy of the real thing.' His face was lined with concern. 'Kerrith must have collected the printout. Now she knows what kind of thing we're looking at.'

'I don't like the sound of all this,' said Smithies again.

'So, I was thinking,' said Tandi. 'Someone needs to look into what's happened to Evie and Miss Longman. And check on Mr Willer in Chepstow. Try and track them down, I mean.'

'Who?' asked Brodie. She hated the thought of the team splitting up.

'Me,' said Tandi quietly.

'Hold on a minute,' insisted Hunter. 'Go off on your own . . . ?'

'I wouldn't be on my own. Fabyan says he'll come with me.' Tandi looked across the room at the American billionaire who was staring intently at a speck of dust on his boots. She was aware her suggestion wasn't receiving the most supportive response from the others. 'Look, my skill on the team was really to take care of everyone. You can see that.'

'What, and we don't need caring for now?' asked Tusia.

'People have gone missing! Maybe because of us. Is it very caring to ignore that and do nothing about it?'

'But it might be dangerous,' urged Hunter.

'We'd be careful. Never out of touch with the team.'

'And what about Kitty?' said Brodie. 'How does she fit in?'

'She can take my place here,' said Tandi. 'She may not have any special skills we know about yet. And she might even fail any tests on code-cracking we choose to give her. But you've got to admit she's brave. Besides, another woman on board has to be a good idea.'

'What, even a woman who smashed the place up?' asked Hunter.

'She was keen to make an impression,' defended Sheldon.

'She certainly did that. You really think we should give Chaos a go?'

'If you've given her one of your nicknames then she's part of the team already,' smiled Brodie.

'It'll be great,' said Sheldon.

Brodie hoped, more than anything, he was right.

'OK,' said Tandi purposefully. 'We need to make sure she knows everything we do about the code before I leave you and go back to London.'

'I don't know how we'll manage without you,' said Smithies.

'Oh, you won't,' joked Tandi. 'I mean, not properly. But the time has come,' she said. 'You know I'm right.'

Let's Tell You What We Know

'Once we've explained everything, there'll be no going back,' said Smithies, fiddling nervously with his tie. 'You're absolutely sure you want to be part of what we're doing here?'

Kitty McCloud rubbed her hands together. 'I'm totally sure,' she said. 'Whatever you're up to's got to be better than working in a pub, and if you think you want me in on the deal, then excellent. Especially after, you know, the damage to the windows and everything.'

Brodie had hoped Kitty wouldn't mention that again.

'Brodie's best at explaining things,' said Smithies. 'She'll tell you all about what's happened here at Station X so far.'

Brodie made her way to the front of the room where various notes and charts had been hidden with covers. Sheldon helped her remove them, then took his seat again.

'It started with a five-hundred-year-old book no one could read,' she said. 'This man called Voynich found it, hidden in a castle in 1912. A letter was sent here to Bletchley Park Mansion and it had a code in it. We thought that might help us read these weird shapes from the book. So we called the letter "the Firebird Code" and we worked together to solve it. And that took us to a place called Brighton and a royal palace and a silver box filled with ash. Except the box had another secret. It was actually a music box which played a tune. Granddad recognised the tune. He knew Elgar had written it. So we guessed the great composer must be linked with the unreadable book.'

'So that's why you came to the Elgar Museum and took the letters and the map?' said Kitty.

'Yes. And we solved more clues hidden by Elgar in a secret message he wrote to his friend Dorabella. This message led us to another book which was saved from a fire centuries before and we thought *that* book was the key to solving the unreadable writing in MS 408.'

'But it wasn't?' Kitty eyes were narrowed in concentration.

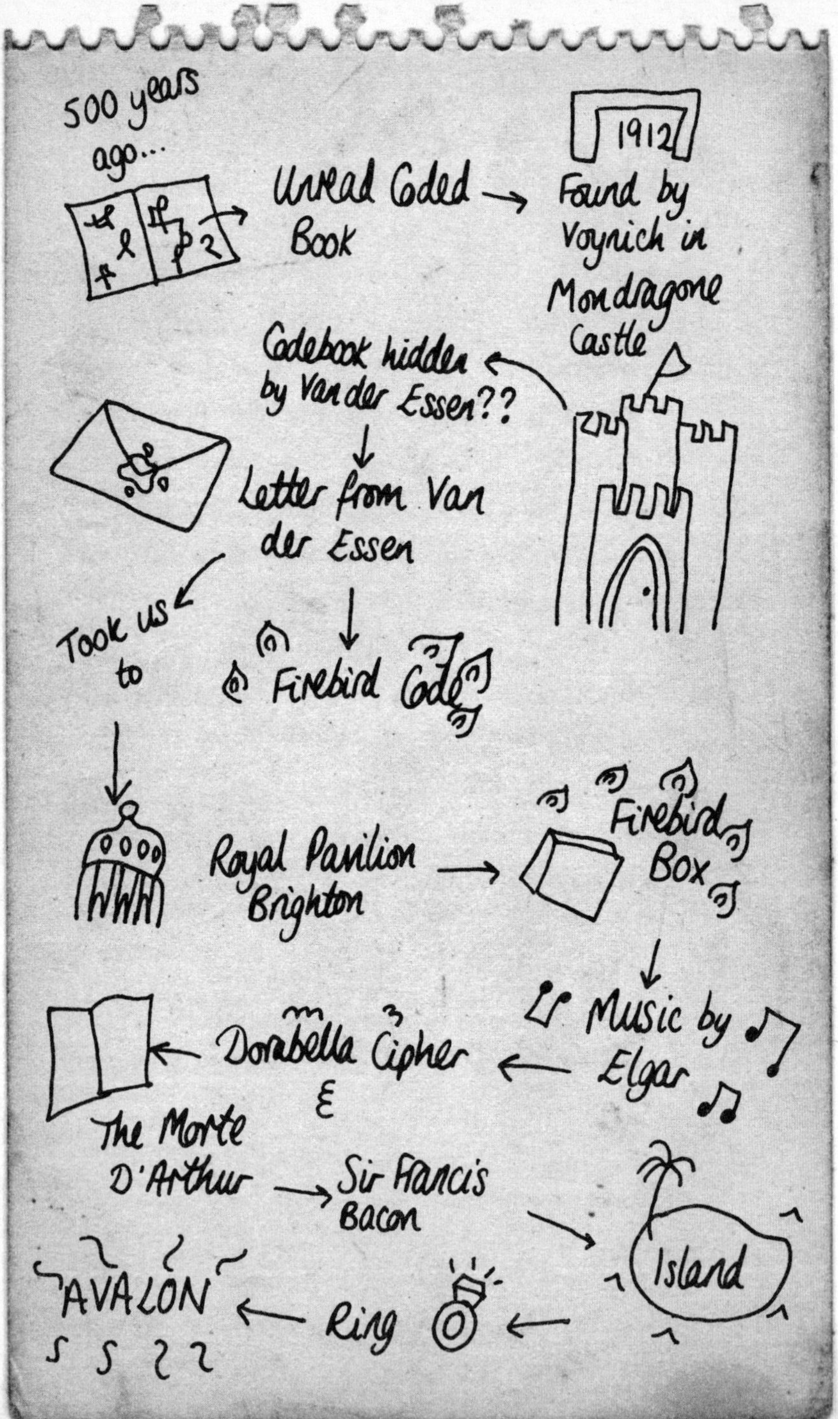
500 years ago...
Unread Coded Book
1912
Found by Voynich in Mondragone Castle
Codebook hidden by Van der Essen??
Letter from Van der Essen
Took us to
Firebird Code
Royal Pavilion Brighton
Firebird Box
Music by Elgar
Dorabella Cipher &
The Morte D'Arthur
Sir Francis Bacon
Island
Ring
AVALON

Brodie shook her head. 'The book was called *Morte D'Arthur*. It had a hidden message too and when we worked out what that said we ended up with the name of one of the greatest writers of all time.'

'Shakespeare?' guessed Kitty.

'No. Not him,' interrupted Hunter, 'but he was important on the way.'

'The writer was a man called Sir Francis Bacon,' carried on Brodie. 'He wrote about an island where amazing things happened. Sir Francis had hidden a ring in the River Wye and we sort of took the ring apart and found another code. And we think this linked back to MS 408.'

'And?' said Kitty, her eagerness mirroring the sense of urgency Brodie had felt as they'd tried to fit the many pieces of the puzzle together.

'The code from Sir Francis's ring made us think MS 408 was the story of a real island. Avalon.'

'I thought Avalon was made up. Part of the story about King Arthur and his knights,' said Kitty.

'So did we,' continued Brodie. 'But everything we've found makes us think Avalon's a real place. There's a special group of people descended from Sir Bedivere who was one of Arthur's Knights of the Round Table. He formed a secret society of people to try and keep the real Avalon a secret. They only told a few people about it.'

'And who are the few?'

Brodie pointed again at the display behind her, jabbing her finger at three columns of names recorded underneath the symbols of a Phoenix, a Griffin and a Branch.

'They're called the Knights of Neustria. We think they've left other coded messages for us to find.'

'And if you find these messages? And you break the codes?' asked Kitty softly.

'Then we read the full story in the unreadable book. And then,' Brodie looked around the room at her friends who, like Kitty, hung on her every word, 'maybe we find Avalon.'

'What's all that?'

Smithies was cutting across the hallway and making for the ballroom. 'A little light reading,' he called over his shoulder.

Sicknote raised his eyebrows.

'Stuff on Avalon.'

Sicknote hurried to hold the ballroom door open and followed Smithies inside.

'Want to check things.' Smithies put the books down on the table.

'You don't think all the clues we've followed point to Avalon?'

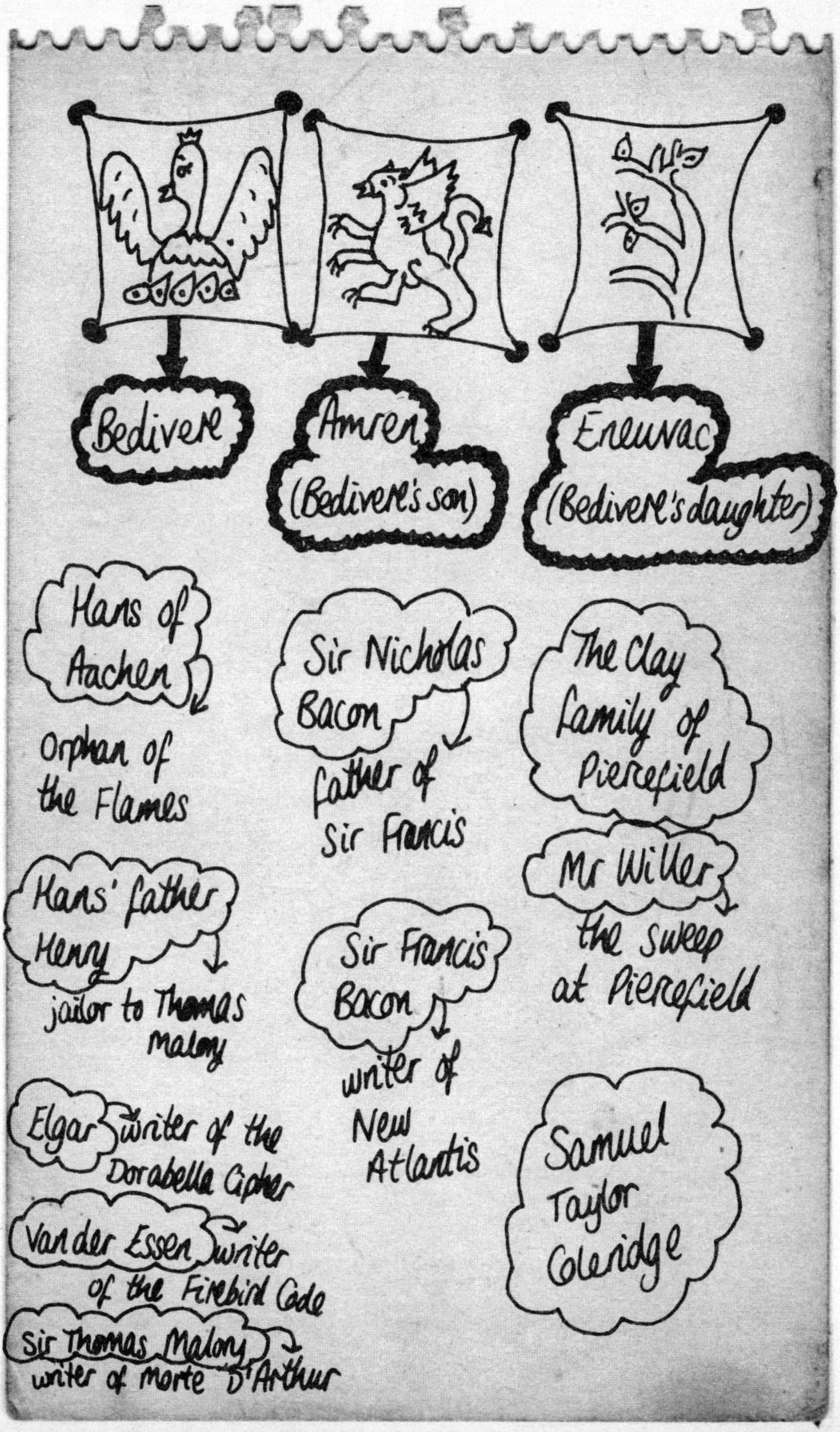
Bedivere
Amren
(Bedivere's son)
Eneuvac
(Bedivere's daughter)
Hans of Aachen
Orphan of the Flames
Sir Nicholas Bacon
father of Sir Francis
The Clay family of Piercefield
Hans' father Henry
jailor to Thomas Malory
Mr Willer
the sweep at Piercefield
Sir Francis Bacon
writer of New Atlantis
Elgar
writer of the Dorabella Cipher
Van der Essen
writer of the Firebird Code
Sir Thomas Malory
writer of Morte D'Arthur
Samuel Taylor Coleridge

'Come on, Oscar. You know as well as I do, there's nothing certain about any of this. But of course I think everything leads to Avalon. I just want to be sure about what Avalon is.'

'Ah. The "magic" idea we talked about when we first broke the code on the Knights of Neustria ring.'

'I'm not sure the kids really get it yet. About the magic protecting ideas. I hope the magic's not a distraction.'

'It's an addition to the stories,' said Sicknote. 'To explain what's really there. That's how stories work, isn't it? Take what exists then try and explain it to us in a way we'll understand.'

'I want to get my head round what might really be at Avalon. So I can help them understand.'

'And what d'you hope all these will help you find?' Sicknote pointed to the pile of books on the table.

'A different kind of magic.'

'We did the right thing to tell her.' Fabyan was leaning against the open door of the stables, petting the neck of one of the zebras.

Brodie offered some grass in the flat of her hand. Another zebra nuzzled her palm and scoffed the treat down quickly.

'The more time we spend on the problem the more

complicated I realise it is,' added Fabyan, stamping his red leather boots. 'I've got a good feeling about this girl Kitty. After all, we need as much help as we can get tracking down other Knights of Neustria.'

'But we *have* found out new things,' said Brodie.

The American nodded half-heartedly. 'But it looks like our progress hasn't gone unnoticed.'

Brodie rubbed the smear of grass juice from her hands. 'Do you think Level Five will try to stop us again?' she asked.

'To be honest, Brodie, I'm not sure why they haven't tracked us more closely. The manuscript's banned. It's obvious we're not supposed to touch it. There was the explosion at your house but then they sort of cooled things down, didn't they? But maybe there's a plan behind letting us find out all we can. I thought they tracked us so carefully at the beginning just to get Friedman out of the picture. But I think I'm wrong.' He hesitated for a moment.

'It's OK,' Brodie said. 'You can talk about him, you know.'

'Betrayal takes a long time to get over,' he said. 'If you ever can.'

Brodie wondered if he was really talking about her and Friedman or whether he was actually talking about the wife she knew had left him one night years ago.

23

Smithies had told them all about it. Fabyan never mentioned it himself.

He stroked the neck of the zebra. 'Don't be like me, Brodie,' he said. 'Don't leave it so late the damage is irreversible. Things aren't usually as simple as they seem.'

She scuffed the ground with the toe of her shoe and the zebra jabbed her shoulder with his muzzle. She reached up and ruffled the black and white coat. There was something so unbelievably fascinating about these strange animals. She wondered if they were really white horses with dark markings or black animals with flashes of white. And then she wondered if it mattered. If being one or another would make a difference to how she felt about them or to what they were.

She realised Fabyan was watching her. 'I tried to contact Friedman this morning,' she said. 'The number he sent weeks ago. He never answers it.'

'So you keep trying.'

'What if he's joined them, though? Maybe now I know about what he did to my mum, he's changed sides. Or gone back to the side he was really on in the first place?'

'Perhaps Tandi and I can find out what's happened to him,' he said softly, 'while we're working on the outside. But will you want to know whatever we find out? Even if it's bad news?'

Brodie didn't know how to answer.

He waited for a while before he broke the silence. 'Will you do something, Brodie? Look after a few things for me?'

'Your zebras?' she said.

'I'm not sure how long we'll be gone. When things or people go missing there's no rules about how long they take to find. We'll come back now and then to check on things your granddad adds to the Listening Post. And I've asked Gordon at the railway station to check in when he can, on the animals, in case you need to leave Station X to follow any leads. But I want you to watch the team while I'm gone,' he mumbled.

'Me?' Brodie said nervously.

A golden tooth glinted in the American's grin. But his eyes were serious, as if he had no doubt in her at all, even if she did.

'And you're totally sure they weren't suspicious?' Kerrith Vernan, as one of the most senior employees in the Government Black Chamber Level Five, had been set the task of 'following things up' at Bletchley. She was determined to make sure everything had gone to plan. Her plan.

The workman shook his head. 'They didn't have a clue,' he grinned.

Kerrith winced a little. The man's smile was irregular. His teeth slightly yellowed. It unsettled her to see such disfigurement so closely. She swallowed and turned her head.

'And what range will the devices have?' she asked tartly.

'Oh, the device on the bike will work for miles,' he said. 'And the monitoring device we attached to the repaired window will pick up everything they say in that room.'

'Good,' said Kerrith without turning.

The man waited, clearly expecting a little more praise for his actions.

Kerrith swatted her hand towards him as if she were driving away an irritating wasp from a picnic. 'That'll do,' she said. 'Now things can begin to get interesting.'

'Who are all those people?' The team met in Hut 11 and Kitty was pointing at a line of photographs and sketches tacked to a display board on the wall.

No one was in a hurry to answer her.

Fabyan and Tandi had left Station X together that morning and the mood of the rest of the team wasn't good. Tandi had tried hard to make them feel it was no big deal, and Fabyan had sung some strange American battle hymn which made them laugh. Now things no longer seemed funny.

'Look, you lot need to try and focus on the job in hand,' said Kitty loudly. 'I know you're going to find it hard with those two gone, but won't it make their efforts kind of pointless if we don't get on with things here?'

'What's with the new kid?' hissed Hunter. 'She needs to know her place.'

'She's got a point though,' said Brodie. 'I mean, we can't sit here moping all the time.'

Hunter shrugged and munched on the stack of toast he'd brought with him from breakfast.

'So these people,' said Kitty, trying again. 'Who are they?'

'Anyone we think's connected to the Knights of Neustria,' Tusia explained. 'People who've left behind some sort of code. Or those we think might've done, if we could find it.'

'They look kind of ancient.'

'Some of them are,' mumbled Hunter.

'But that's Elgar, right?' Kitty said, pointing at a picture of a man with a rather fine moustache. 'Know him from the museum back home.'

'So you remember this is Jaegar, then,' said Sheldon,

gesturing to another photo. 'His music publisher. The man who sent the letters. Elgar wrote one of the *Enigma Variations* about him.'

Kitty moved further along the line.

'If these people were all Knights of Neustria,' went on Brodie, 'and they promised to keep the secrets about Avalon, then we're thinking they may have more information stored somewhere – about what they knew. That's what we need to find next.'

'You mean in some sort of secret record?' Kitty asked.

'Maybe,' agreed Tusia. 'I mean, the Knights weren't all alive at the same time. So they must have had ways of passing on information to new members. We've found some of them: coded rings; musical boxes; letters to friends; but we've only got half the story.'

'We still can't read MS 408 and we still don't know where Avalon is.' Brodie didn't feel good saying this out loud. 'So we're trying to fill in the gaps in what we know.'

'I get it,' said Kitty. 'But why d'you choose this place to hang out? Not that it isn't great to be working in a stately home and doing research in a garden shed and everything. It's just, it's not sort of cutting edge, is it? Not very modern.'

'You tell her, Smithies,' urged Tusia.

'Station X is the home of codes,' he explained. 'It was a code-cracking centre in World War Two. Then years later another Team Veritas met here in secret to try and make sense of MS 408. My parents were here. I lived with them while they worked on the code.'

'I was here too,' cut in Mr Bray, 'with my wife and Brodie's mum. And there were others.' He fiddled with the cuff of his shirt. 'Back then it wasn't seen as such a good idea to get kids involved in solving codes.'

'But we've moved on since then,' said Smithies. 'Code-crackers used to be chosen from the best minds at university. We have a different system now.'

Kitty traced the edge of the photograph board with her finger. 'But I bet you've got to be mega clever to be able to crack codes, haven't you?' she said nervously. 'Cos I'm not brainy. And these Knights of Neustria – they were clever, right?'

'Cracking codes is really about making connections,' said Tusia slowly. 'But yes, some of them were really clever.' She stood up and walked in front of the photos. 'You know, you might be on to something there, Kitty. Bletchley's midway between Oxford and Cambridge universities, isn't it, Smithies?'

'It's one of the reasons the mansion was chosen.'

'So I wonder how many of the Knights of Neustria had links there. With Oxford and Cambridge, I mean.

If we're looking for a place where the Knights of Neustria met years ago to pass on ideas, maybe it was at one of them.'

Hunter looked excited suddenly. 'Bacon went to Cambridge University, remember? Got in when he was only twelve . . .'

'And what about Coleridge?' said Sheldon, moving down the line of Knights tacked behind them.

'Cambridge too,' smiled Sicknote. 'Sort of detail I like to know about a person.'

'So,' said Brodie, 'Coleridge and Bacon. The two Knights who wore the special rings were both students at Cambridge University. Do you think that's important?'

'Maybe other Knights of Neustria studied there?' added Hunter. 'Passed on information to each other through a secret club?'

'They're called societies,' said Granddad enthusiastically. 'Universities have lots of them. I remember reading about something called the Society of Dilettanti that started at Cambridge. Someone called Thomas Anson set it up. They studied other cultures. They liked ancient Greek art.'

'And was it secret?' asked Brodie.

'Not really. Just hard to join. But I guess there were secret societies as well.'

'So maybe there was one which passed on stories and codes from the Knights of Neustria. But it must have had a different name, that's why we can't find out about it in any of the history books.' Brodie mulled the thought over. 'What d'you think? If you were going to leave more clues about something as important as finding Avalon, then surely an ancient university's the place to do it.'

'Let's look into it,' said Tusia excitedly. 'We need another code to follow. Another secret message to decipher to help add to the clues about Avalon. And if some of our Knights went to Cambridge University, then that seems like a great place to start!'

'So we're going to Cambridge?' said Kitty, her eyes wide in anticipation.

Sicknote looked like he was going to burst. 'No we are not!'

'We've been to Cambridge before. It didn't go well,' explained Hunter.

'Oh, I don't know,' cut in Sheldon. 'We got our answers, didn't we? That Miss Jarratt knew her stuff.'

'*That* Miss Jarratt led us into a whole load of danger,' grumbled Sicknote.

'But surely it's worth asking her. We'd be careful. Extra careful. Come on. We've got a link with someone in Cambridge who might know what we need.'

Brodie looked from Sicknote to Granddad. Then she fixed her gaze determinedly on Smithies.

'OK,' he said at last, holding up his hands. 'Let's get in touch with Miss Jarratt. But I'm not altogether sure we should be dealing with someone who sends us wooden spoons.'

There were no wooden spoons. This time Miss Jarratt sent them a metal fork and a watch.

'She's totally bonkers,' groaned Tusia, picking up the watch and looking carefully. 'It's not even working,' she added. 'Look, the time's stuck on 3.00 p.m. The date on February 10th.' She shook the watch beside her ear but there was obviously no ticking.

'This is a present?' mused Kitty, pulling a rather odd face.

'No. It's a code,' explained Sheldon. 'That's how Miss Jarratt works.'

'What does she want us to do?' grinned Hunter. 'Eat the watch with the fork? Because even I would struggle with that.'

Tusia's eyes widened. 'Eat time!' she yelped. 'That's it. I know what this means. I know exactly where we have to go and when.'

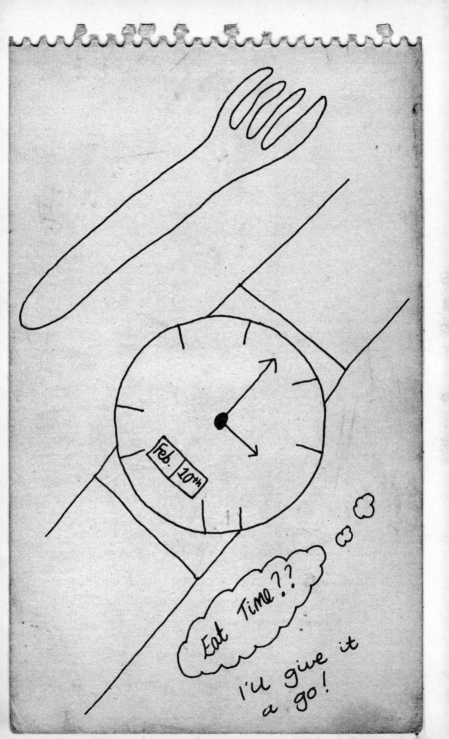

The Cambridge Apostles

'It's called the Chronophage,' said Tusia. 'It means "time eater".'

'I think it's weird,' said Sheldon.

It was ten to three on the 10th February and the team were standing outside the Corpus Clock on the side of the Taylor Library at Corpus Christi College, Cambridge. Sheldon had a point. The clock was weird. But Brodie loved it.

'It's telling a story,' she said as she watched the huge metal grasshopper at the top of the enormous golden clock face move forward slowly as if it was munching its way through the edge of the dial. The clock had no hands. Instead, lights flashed inside the dials to show the seconds, minutes and hours. Every now and then the grasshopper blinked its eyes.

They stood in silence in front of the clock as the lights flickered. Then there was a rattling noise like a chain being dropped into a coffin as the lights blazed three o'clock.

'Inside the church!' urged a voice suddenly from behind them. 'It's safer there.' Miss Jarratt led the way into the tiny St Bene't's church and made sure the door was closed behind her. 'This way,' she said, hurrying forward.

She strode to the back of the church and clicked open a door built into a huge stone pillar. A spiral staircase twisted upwards and Miss Jarratt ushered them on to the first few steps. 'I have little time,' she said, and Brodie remembered the grasshopper on the clock eating frantically.

'Miss Jarratt,' began Smithies. 'You were good to meet with us again. Your help last time, passing on what Zimansky knew, was extremely important to us and—'

'You know you're not safe here?'

Smithies held on to the banister of the curling stairs. 'Miss Jarratt, we've come to the conclusion that we aren't safe anywhere. Our job is to find answers before it's too late. Before time runs out.'

'And you need more answers about MS 408?'

'We just need to know about secret societies in Cambridge,' Brodie insisted.

Miss Jarratt's eyes sparkled even in the gloom. 'Ahh. You want to know about the apostles. I knew you'd want to know eventually.'

'The apostles?' said Hunter. 'That was part of your last clue to us, wasn't it? The twelve apostles. It was how we knew to wash the stone you gave us to show the hidden message.'

Miss Jarratt smiled. 'You did well to make that connection, but if you're after secret societies then you should be looking beyond the apostles in the Bible. You need to think about the Cambridge Apostles.'

'Who?'

'A secret group based here at the university. We only began to learn about their existence a while ago.'

'It's a religious thing?' asked Hunter.

'No. A bookish thing. The group formed in 1820 and originally it was called the Apostles as there were only twelve members. Once you graduated from Cambridge you could become something called an Angel.'

'So who belonged?' Brodie asked.

'Well, some of the most modern members of the society have been rather expert code-crackers. Not in a good way, I'm afraid,' she added quickly. 'Some of them went on to use their code-cracking skills to work as spies. In the 1950s a group were revealed called the Cambridge Five. They were all Cambridge Apostles.'

Brodie looked across at Smithies. It was obvious he knew the story but Miss Jarratt was allowing no time for explanations.

'We shouldn't judge them,' Sicknote interjected from the bottom of the stairs. 'I don't think any of us are in a position to question those who work against the wishes of a government. Let's just go with the idea these people knew lots about codes and secrets.'

'So the Apostles, then,' said Tusia, 'were set up to learn about codes?'

'Oh no,' said Miss Jarratt. 'Codes didn't come into it. They were set up to look at the work of Samuel Taylor Coleridge.'

Sicknote made a whistling noise between his teeth. Brodie beamed.

'You've been very helpful, Miss Jarratt,' said Smithies.

'And you've been rather reckless,' she said. She peered out of the doorway into the church. 'I'm not sure Cambridge is safe for you.'

'I'm sure it's not,' said Smithies. 'But Cambridge has the answers we need.'

* * *

Cambridge Apostles → Formed in 1820

↓

Twelve members

1950s

Cambridge 5 Spy Ring

O

When you left you became an angel

I'm liking all these numbers

Group formed to look at the work of

Samuel Taylor Coleridge

Cambridge Apostles = Cover for the Knights of Neustria

♡ ✷
✦ ✤

They were seated in the RAF bar of the Eagle pub, sipping lemonades and sharing bags of pickled onion crisps. Tusia was finding it hard to concentrate because of the graffiti all over the ceiling.

'Oi,' snapped Hunter, through a mouthful of crisps. 'Eyes off the World War Two scribbling and get your mind back on the Cambridge Apostles.' He opened a second bag. 'It sounds right, doesn't it? A perfect cover for Knights of Neustria.'

'An organisation meeting in secret with a select group of members. I like it,' said Brodie.

'It's like us,' said Sheldon. 'Select, I mean. All chosen for a reason. Our skill with codes. The thing we have in common.'

Kitty shuffled on her chair.

'So let's think about the other members of the Apostles, then,' said Brodie. 'Are there any more Apostles who could have been Knights?' Sicknote smoothed a piece of paper flat on the table. It was a printout of the members of the Cambridge Apostles he'd managed to get from the Taylor Library computer after quite a lot of bargaining with the librarian. 'Any names jump out at you? Anything that might link them to Avalon?'

Even Hunter stopped munching. The room was quiet.

Then Brodie jabbed the list with her finger. 'Him,' she said.

Tandi and Fabyan stood outside the chip shop. The rain had eased but it was still cold. Tandi pulled her coat higher around her shoulders.

'I shouldn't be doing this.'

'Nothing will go wrong, Les,' Tandi said quite forcibly.

The cleaner from the Black Chamber didn't look too sure.

'We just need to find a way to get me inside the Black Chamber so I can try and set up a remote access to the computers.'

'Oh, is that all!'

Tandi patted his shoulder. 'Look. I know it sounds huge. But let's take it step by step. Can you get me back inside the building?'

'I guess. A security card. It'll work the doors. You just scan yourself in, like you used to.'

'OK. My card will have been blocked, of course. But you could get hold of another card?'

'Yes. But then the rest is ridiculous. How on earth would you get on the computers? Your security would have been revoked. It's all password protected. Even the cleaners know that.'

'And even the cleaners know there's always a way round things. When you're dealing with people.'

'But you're not dealing with people, are you?' choked Les. 'We're talking computers.'

'Operated by people, Les. Human error. That's got to play a part.'

'No, you've lost me. Don't know what you're talking about.'

Fabyan reached into his pocket and pulled out his wallet. It was bulging with bank-notes. 'Human error, Les. People make mistakes all the time. And very often this is the reason.'

'Money?'

'Money. And power, I guess.'

'I still don't follow.'

'We need you to think very hard about the people who work in that building. Not the ones with real power . . . but the ones who long for power. And then the ones who long for money. And when you've come up with someone who wants both, then we have our way in.'

'But that Vernan woman's been on to me before. Made me give away stuff about Friedman.'

Tandi felt a little sick. 'You know about Robbie? Why he hasn't come back?'

'I just do my job, miss. I don't want any trouble.'

'That doesn't stop trouble finding us,' said Tandi. 'Please, Les. I need to get back inside the Black Chamber. You have to help.'

'Nice place you've got here.'

The barman smiled and Kerrith twisted her diamond ring around her finger. It prevented her from touching any of the surfaces in the Eagle pub that were bound to be sticky with beer.

'Great discoveries made in this pub,' said the barman proudly. 'Crick and Watson announced they'd figured out their scientific theory about how DNA worked here one lunchtime.'

'Nice.' Kerrith did not lower her hands. 'You have several groups who meet to chat, then?' she said.

'Bar's always busy,' he added. 'And they tell me students have no money. The RAF bar at the back gets even busier than this one. Cambridge types like their history, see.'

It was the first time Kerrith had allowed herself to smile.

The barman twisted a white cloth around the inside of a pint glass but when he turned back to pick up another one, the woman had gone.

The piece of paper was crumpled in the middle of a sea

of abandoned crisp packets. It made Kerrith feel physically sick to reach amongst them. She held the paper with two fingers and allowed it to flap from one corner. She could see all she needed. The name 'Alfred Tennyson' circled in red.

'What you doing?'

Brodie looked up from her chair in the corner of the library. She was not in the mood to talk to Kitty. Everyone was still cross with her because of the mistake she'd made in Cambridge. Kitty had been trusted with bringing the list of the Apostles home and she'd lost it. She was sure she'd put it in the pocket of her leather bike trousers but she couldn't find it. Smithies had told them all to let it go. Brodie was finding it hard. The new girl needed to understand the danger they were up against.

'What you doing?' Kitty asked again.

Brodie peered over the top of the dusty green book she was holding. Kitty was standing in the doorway to the library clutching something tight.

'Erm, reading,' said Brodie, who was entirely sure no one had ever asked her that question before. They'd asked her *what* she was reading. They'd asked her *how good* what she was reading was. They'd asked her if *she'd nearly finished*. But as far as she could remember, no one had ever asked her *what* she was doing.

'Oh,' said Kitty.

'It's Tennyson,' Brodie said. 'I thought I'd look again at what he'd written about King Arthur, what with him being a Cambridge Apostle and everything. And how he wrote about Avalon.'

'You've read his stuff before though?'

Brodie tried not to frown. This girl really didn't understand about reading.

'But you're looking again because he was one of these Apostles?'

Brodie tried to answer calmly. 'I think he might have been a Knight of Neustria and so he might have left us some clues.'

'And has he?'

Brodie laughed. 'It usually takes a while to find them.'

'Oh.'

Brodie was just going to explain that people before her had given their whole lives over to trying to find clues about MS 408 when she became distracted by whatever Kitty was holding. 'What's that?' she said.

'Oh, this,' said Kitty, moving further into the room. 'I found it in the music room. Some ornament or something.' The wooden statue of an elephant wobbled in her palm.

'It's the Jumbo Rush Elephant,' Brodie said.

'The what?'

'It was here in the Second World War. The code-crackers would get it out of the cupboard and put it on their desks when there was a vital code to crack. When they thought people might die if they didn't crack that code.'

Kitty moved the elephant backwards and forwards. 'And you still keep it?' she said.

'This place is all about history and danger.'

Kitty put the elephant on the table. 'Can I?' she said, gesturing to a chair beside Brodie.

'Sure.'

Kitty sat down. 'You know, in my family we've got an expression.' She ran her finger along the back of the wooden statue as she spoke. 'We talk about the elephant in the room. D'you know what that means?'

Brodie knew, but something about the way Kitty asked the question made her feel she should let Kitty explain.

'It's when there's something important or awkward not being mentioned or discussed.' She took her hand away from the statue. 'There's a lot of elephants here at Bletchley, Brodie.'

Brodie felt the weight of the book on her knee. 'Really. You think?'

'Sure. There's the whole thing with Sicknote and the pyjamas. What's that all about?'

'It's just the way he dresses.'

'And Smithies always dashing off to get home.'

'His wife isn't well.'

'And the biggest elephant of all has to be how weird you are whenever anyone mentions this Friedman guy.'

Brodie felt the pages of her book against the tips of her fingers. The sharp edge of the paper felt reassuring. 'It's complicated.'

'Sure. Most problems are.'

Brodie didn't say anything.

'I think it's odd, that's all. But I suppose I'm not like you lot.'

'What d'you mean?'

'Well, you all have your thing. Your issues.'

'We have our special skills if that's what you're on about?'

Kitty shuffled back on the chair. 'They're issues.'

'I don't understand.'

'Well, there's Hunter with his whole number thing. That's got to be about trying to make things add up in his head, when everything seems off balance. And Tusia and her shape and space thing, that's about control, right. Having things her way. And Sheldon. His music was always an escape, and having worked at the Plough for so long I totally get why he does that.'

Brodie wasn't sure whether to be horrified at Kitty's bluntness or impressed. 'And me? What's my issue?'

'Apart from the Friedman thing?' Kitty reached out and tapped the book on her lap. 'Oh, you're looking for your happy ending, aren't you? Trying to make sense of your own story.'

Brodie felt the hairs on the back of her neck bristle. 'I don't think you can really just turn up here and think you know all about us.'

'Oh, it's fine for you to ignore it. But I'm just saying it as it is. I'm just telling you about the elephants.'

Brodie pressed her fingers hard against the pages of the book. 'So what's your issue then, if you're so keen to find out ours?'

'Me? An eighteen-year-old barmaid, who's answerable to no one? I don't have issues.'

'OK. So what's your "thing"?' pressed Brodie.

Kitty shrugged. 'Well, it's not brains, that's for sure.'

'You have a problem with us being clever?'

'I never said it was a problem.'

Brodie frowned.

'But I don't see why you've asked me to join you. I don't know how I could possibly help.'

'We asked you because you took a risk to find us. Because you brought us the letters.'

'Which no one has even looked at again, by the way.'

Brodie felt a burning in her cheeks. 'I'm sorry,' she said. 'We tend to do that. Get sidetracked, I mean. Follow different leads. We *will* look at them. It was important you brought them.'

'Really?'

Brodie remembered it was one of the reasons Tandi was so keen to let Kitty stay. 'We can look at them now, if you like.' She put the Tennyson book down on the floor. 'My happy ending can wait for a while. Why don't you go and get them?'

Kitty drew a wad of papers from her sleeve.

'You had them with you all along?' said Brodie.

'Well, I knew I had to make you feel bad before you put that crazy book down. From what everyone here tells me, when you get stuck in a story it takes drastic measures to pull you out!' She shook the roll of papers flat. 'So. Jaeger to Elgar. Evie thought they were important.'

Brodie swept her hair behind her shoulders and flexed her hands before taking the first letter.

'That's the one she seemed most keen I kept safe. He wrote it sometime after 1905, so Evie said.' Kitty narrowed her eyes in concentration. 'What do you think?'

4

Blackmail at the Black Chamber

It was a strange letter. It had obviously been written when Jaeger was unwell. Brodie read the section aloud.

'When I think over it all, and realise how beautiful life is and what work I might do and what intellectual beauty (E's symphony) there is still brought forth by men of genius – and how very soon I shall be dead to it all, dead to family and friends and Sunshine and green fields and quartets and poetry and pictures and all that makes life the great thing it is, then my heart feels heavy, heavy as lead, and tears flow readily.'

There was nothing there – she was sure. But maybe she wasn't looking hard enough. Maybe she was dismissing it too soon. She stared again, focusing hard as if trying to draw the secret from the page. Then something clicked into place. 'That's it,' she yelped. She prodded the letter excitedly with her finger. 'What d'you notice? About the way he's written "Sunshine"?'

Kitty had no answer.

'Look!' Brodie urged, pushing the paper forward. 'Tusia would have got this in a minute.'

'Shape and Space?' said Kitty.

Brodie nodded.

Kitty leant in closer. 'OK. Sunshine. Oh, OK. I see it. He's used a capital letter.'

'Exactly,' shouted Brodie. 'In the middle of a sentence where it doesn't need a capital. He's making it important. The light's important. The light of knowledge. So we have to think about what words he uses near the word Sunshine. They'll be the things we have to look at to find answers.'

She peered in closer and then took a pencil and made a numbered list.

1. Green Fields

2. Quartets

3. Poetry

4. Pictures

She scored neatly under each word. 'Maybe when we think about the Cambridge Apostles and the Knights of Neustria we should look for these four things. Might help us find more information about MS 408.'

Kitty's grin widened.

'And I think somehow we need to make a connection back to Elgar.'

'Why?'

'Because this letter with the clues was written to Elgar. He wrote the Arthur music. He left us the Dorabella Cipher. I think there's things Elgar's still got to tell us.'

'So you want to find connections between him and other Knights?' mused Kitty. 'Maybe with other Cambridge Apostles?'

'I think so,' said Brodie. 'Our job here's all about making connections. We've been taught that from the very beginning.'

'So which Apostle do you think we should start with, then?'

The answer was obvious.

Tandi adjusted her jacket, twisted the button at her cuff and then eased the short cropped wig a little lower down her forehead.

'Ready?' said Fabyan.

'No. But we have to do this.'

'OK. Nice and steady. Try not to look too nervous. But try not to look too confident either. Sort of in the middle. Relaxed. But not too relaxed.'

'Will you please—'

'Sorry. I was just . . . trying to help.'

Tandi did up the button on her cuff again.

'Got the pass?' said Fabyan.

Tandi fiddled at the lanyard tucked inside her jacket. Les's borrowed security card felt heavy somehow round her neck. But they'd worked everything through. The plan was simple. If it worked it would be brilliant. If it failed then things would go desperately wrong. They'd got no choice. 'OK. I'm going in.'

Fabyan nodded. 'Good luck!'

'And why exactly do you think I'd be interested?' Kerrith squinted across her polished desk. She could barely see the man properly but she wouldn't give him the satisfaction of seeing her wear glasses. 'Well? I'm waiting?'

The man at the other side of the desk shuffled nervously. The polish on his pointed shoes reflected the light. 'You just said we were to keep you up to date with any unexpected book sales or purchases, of a,' he coughed to clear his throat, 'sensitive nature.'

'And?'

The man shuffled again.

'Oh, for goodness' sake, spit it out, Wheeler. What do you know and why do I need to know it?'

'It was in Chepstow, ma'am. A beggar by all accounts, trying to have a first edition book valued.'

'And did he sell the book, this beggar?' Her lips stumbled over the final word as if she thought using it would contaminate her in some way.

'No, ma'am. That's what drew our attention.'

'Go on.' Kerrith was growing decidedly impatient.

'The man had a first edition of Coleridge poems. It had an inscription too, linking it to a wealthy family of the time. And yet, despite being told how much the book would fetch,' Kerrith's eyes sparkled with anticipation, 'he simply left the shop without attempting to haggle.'

Kerrith ran her finger across her lip. 'Chepstow, you say?'

'Yes, ma'am.'

'And the man is traceable and easily removed?'

'Oh, absolutely, ma'am. By all accounts he lives on a derelict site and will be missed by no one.' He hunched his shoulders, scared of the impact his words would have. 'Should we bring him in to Down Street, ma'am?'

Kerrith leant back on her chair as if picturing a

particularly pleasing scene. 'Do it,' she said. 'No fuss. No trails.'

'Certainly, ma'am.' Wheeler turned to make for the door.

'One other thing,' she said, her hands linked behind her head as she leant back into the comfort of the black leather. 'What's the latest information on Friedman?'

'Word is he's totally broken, ma'am.'

This information made her happy. 'And there's no contact with the outside world? He's not allowed to write?'

Wheeler shook his head.

'And the girl?' Kerrith snarled the words. 'Does she still try and make contact with him?'

'Yes, ma'am. In fact, the phone calls have increased in number.'

'And you tell him she phones?' Kerrith said, enjoying the words like a cat toying with an injured mouse.

'No, ma'am. We tell him nothing.'

Kerrith took her arms away from her head and folded them in front of her. 'That will be all,' she said dismissively.

'OK. So she's gone totally bonkers,' said Sheldon, lowering his flute from his mouth as he led the others into the music room.

'Not *gone*. B was always a tomato short of a salad,' added Hunter, as he stared around the room.

'What's all this?' said Tusia, stepping over the books and papers splayed across the floor and then bending to shuffle them into neater piles. 'Is this the *entire* contents of the library?'

As Brodie surveyed the scene, she knew it could be argued she'd been a bit excessive but somehow she wanted to make the point for Kitty. 'Here, Granddad,' she said, turning once more. 'Why don't you take a seat by the fireplace?'

Smithies joined him, while Sicknote positioned himself beside the window and hastily secured his mug of coffee to the radiator with the end of the long metal chain.

'Well?' said Smithies, pushing his glasses further up the bridge of his nose. 'Are you going to explain?'

'It's the complete work of Tennyson,' Brodie said. 'Well, almost the complete. It's everything I could find in the library.'

'OK,' said Hunter. 'And it's stacked up in piles around the music room, why exactly?'

'Because I think we should read it.'

'Make that a tomato and an uncut cucumber short of a salad,' whispered Hunter behind the cover of his arm.

Tusia looked up from the furthest pile. 'You want us to read it all?' she said, patting the edges of the stack nearest to her and straightening the load. 'Everything?'

Brodie smiled awkwardly.

'Why?'

'Because of Jaeger's letter.'

'You've looked at them?' Hunter did little to hide the surprise in his voice.

'Kitty and I looked at them yesterday evening.'

'I see.' Hunter's voice sounded steely. 'And you didn't think to wait for us?'

'I sort of forced her,' chipped in Kitty. 'She was going to wait but I persuaded her.'

'And you found something?'

'I think we did,' said Brodie. She explained about the use of the word Sunshine in the letter. Then she showed the list.

1. Green Fields

2. Quartets

3. Poetry

4. Pictures

'What if these are the things we should look for to give us answers about Avalon and MS 408? Poems seemed a good place to start. Maybe poems by the Cambridge Apostles. And I just thought Tennyson was perfect for kicking things off. See if we could find a link.'

'Link to what?'

'Back to Elgar.'

Sicknote looked excited. 'You think we missed stuff last time?'

'Maybe. Elgar wrote about Arthur in his music. He could've got scared Dorabella would never understand the cipher he wrote her, so left more clues just in case.'

'But why do you think these extra clues he left were connected to Tennyson?' said Granddad.

'Elgar and Tennyson both told us stories about Arthur,' said Brodie. 'One in music, one in words. What if they told us a story *together* that we haven't found yet?'

Sheldon flopped down to the ground and flicked the pages of the book on the nearest pile. 'It's worth a shot,' he said.

'I knew it would take a while, so I've brought food!' she added triumphantly, wheeling out a trolley packed with cakes and pastries.

'Oh, well, in that case,' said Hunter, reaching to take a custard slice from the plate. 'What we waiting for?'

Brodie joined Sheldon on the floor. 'There's loads of stuff here that probably won't help. We just have to go for it.'

'What's this poem called "Maud"?' Tusia asked, flicking open a book and sharing it with Smithies.

'I'll take "In Memorium",' said Sicknote, sharing his text with Mr Bray. 'I'm particularly fond of poems written about death.'

'Me and Fingers will take this "Lotos-Eaters" thing,' spluttered Hunter, through a mouthful of pastry. 'I'd rather read about food than death, thanks very much.'

'Typical,' hissed Tusia. 'Absolutely typical.'

'What?'

'Do you ever think of anything other than your stomach?'

Hunter shrugged and reached for a chocolate éclair.

Tandi leant her hands on the counter top. Her palms were sweaty. The technician looked up from his screen.

'You see, it's just my clearance status. I don't know. Some sort of gremlin.'

'Gremlin?' The technician couldn't look more patronising if he tried. 'You mean a virus?'

Tandi wiped her palm along the counter. 'Oh, I don't know. Something's not right.'

'Miss, there's loads of people here with IT problems. There's a procedure, you know. A system for fixing glitches. Line manager first and then me. I don't have the authority to—'

'Oh, I know. Procedures, protocol. I get all that. But you see, I've been away. Undercover work.' She winked. 'All high security and on the down low. A black obs number.'

The technician was looking intrigued. 'You for real? They sent you out undercover? High risk, was it?'

'Total high risk. And now for some reason my password won't let me in and—'

'Of course it won't. Passwords change. If you've been out on active service it won't be the same. And as I said I don't have the authority to go giving you new passwords. More than my job's worth.'

'Worth more than this?' Tandi said, taking a large brown envelope from her pocket and sliding it across the counter.

'Now, hold on, lady. What you playing at? I can't be bought, you know. What d'you take me for? You want me to call security?'

Tandi slid the envelope hastily back into her pocket. 'I'm sorry. My mistake. I just thought. You know. Finances as they are.'

The technician was seething. 'Yeah, well, you picked the wrong man, lady.'

Tandi doubted that was true. Les had been very specific. He'd done his research.

'I'm sorry,' said Tandi. 'Just forget I said anything. I'll see my line manager. Get this gremlin sorted and—'

'Yeah. Right. Wrong guy, lady. Understand me?'

Tandi nodded.

The technician leant back in the chair.

Tandi waited. Her palms were wet again.

'Just out of interest . . . how much was it?'

'Five thousand. Used notes.'

The technician whistled softly between his teeth. 'Five thousand pounds, you say?'

'I'm sorry. I should never have suggested anything. It's just I suppose with the economy as it is. Mortgage rates. College fees. I just thought it would save some time.'

'But you've got to be up to no good, lady. Stands to reason.'

'I think the five thousand pounds entitles me to be sure you don't ask questions.'

'No. I'm sorry. More than my job's worth.'

'Which would be true, wouldn't it, if your job wasn't on the line because of the computer products owned by Black Chamber that you've been selling off on the side?'

The technician's skin greyed.

'Shame if that news got out. I mean, if I slipped up for example and told someone.'

'You blackmailing me?'

'Such a nasty word. But yes. I suppose I am.' Tandi took the envelope and put it on the counter again. 'Do we have a deal?

5

Tennyson's Shadow

The trolley was nearly empty of food by the time Brodie had finished reading 'The Day-Dream'. She rubbed her temples and looked around the room. 'Anything?' she said hopefully. 'Anything at all?'

Her question was greeted with silence. Maybe this hadn't been such a good idea. She'd had a wonderful time, and for a while she'd been lost in Tennyson's words. But as for a link with Elgar. She'd drawn a blank.

'I've had enough,' Tusia said apologetically. 'I can't see straight I'm so tired. We can carry on tomorrow.'

'Don't beat yourself up about it,' encouraged Sheldon, standing and wandering over to the sound system. 'Just because we haven't found anything, doesn't mean it's not there.' He reached for the CD. 'Let's have some Elgar to lift the mood. What d'you think?'

'Please not the Arthur music,' said Brodie, a little too keenly. 'Something else.'

'OK,' said Sheldon, skipping through the tracks on the CD. 'What about this? It's called "Sweet Music".'

'Not more food references,' groaned Hunter. 'It was bad enough reading a poem about a group of people who couldn't stop eating!'

Sheldon ignored the protest and pressed play on the CD.

'I'm going to make my way up to my room,' said Granddad, giving Brodie a hug goodnight. 'Don't be too hard on yourself, sweetheart. It was a great idea.'

'Hold on,' a voice pleaded from the corner of the room.

'Sleep well.'

'For the love of all that's chocolate coated, will you please hold on!' yelled Hunter from his seat on the floor.

Brodie held tight to her granddad.

'Stop the CD. Stop it now.'

'OK, mate. No need to have a coronary about it,' moaned Sheldon as he pressed stop.

'What did you say this piece was called?' yelled

Hunter again, fumbling with the pages on the floor. 'Sweet, right? You said it was "Sweet Music".'

'Yes. And then you got all moany about the use of the word "sweet" and once again managed to bring the conversation back round to the needs of your stomach and . . .'

'That's the link!' Hunter ignored Tusia. 'Between Elgar and Tennyson.' He held open the poem book and flapped it in his hands. 'Sweet Music is the title of the chorus part of this poem "The Lotos-Eaters". Elgar must have set that part of Tennyson's work to music. Look.'

CHORAL SECTION OF 'THE LOTOS-EATERS' POEM

There is sweet music here that softer falls
Than petals from blown roses on the grass,
Or night-dews on still waters between walls
Of shadowy granite, in a gleaming pass;
Music that gentlier on the spirit lies,
Than tired eyelids upon tired eyes;
Music that brings sweet sleep down from the blissful skies.
Here are cool mosses deep,
And thro' the moss the ivies creep,
And in the stream the long-leaved flowers weep,
And from the craggy ledge the poppy hangs in sleep.

Brodie leapt forward and grabbed the book. 'And the poem. What's the poem about?' she blurted.

Hunter eased back on his heels and his grin broadened. 'You're going to love it.'

'Why?'

Hunter waited, wanting to be sure everyone in the room was paying maximum attention. 'It's about an incredible island.'

'It's totally brilliant,' giggled Brodie.

'Doesn't she say this about every poem and story she ever reads?' whispered Kitty.

'But it makes sense,' said Brodie, hardly able to contain her enthusiasm. 'Hunter says the poem's about a group of sailors who find this island and eat the fruit there and then don't know whether they should ever leave.'

'So is the island Avalon?' asked Tusia, directing her gaze at Smithies.

'I'm not sure,' he said, resting his glasses on his forehead as he always did when he was thinking. 'Let's work it through.'

'But I thought the excitement of the whole thing was that we might have found a link to MS 408,' demanded Kitty.

'Oh, we may have found a link,' said Smithies. 'But

I'm not sure the island in the poem is Avalon.' He took the poetry book and skimmed the pages. 'It's a while since I read it. But I'm remembering now.'

Everyone shuffled closer to hear.

'OK. Let's take this in stages.' Smithies gestured to the notes above the poem which set the scene. 'The poem's based on something Homer wrote called *the Odyssey*. Homer wrote about this huge storm blowing sailors off course when they were sailing back from the war in Troy. They land on this island and there's these people there who do nothing all day but eat lotos flowers.'

'That's why I liked the poem. Sounds like my sort of place,' joked Hunter, gazing contentedly up at the skylight.

'It starts off OK but eventually everything just feels the same. The men give up wanting to go back to all the things they left behind.'

'So they don't go home, then?' asked Tusia.

Smithies shook his head. 'But perhaps, if this poem links Elgar and Tennyson, we should go with the idea it means one thing to some readers, and something else to Knights of Neustria,' he suggested tentatively.

'Like the fish carved into the tree down by the River Wye when we were hunting for Bacon's ring?' asked Tusia.

66

Kitty looked around for an explanation.

'It meant "fisherman" to some people and "Christian" to others,' Tusia whispered. 'We've found a lot of things that can be understood two ways.'

'And so,' said Smithies, sighing elaborately, 'this poem could mean more than one thing too. It *could be* about Odysseus and his men but it *could also be* about travellers *from* Avalon who arrive somewhere and everything isn't as it seems.'

'Why d'you think the poem could mean the sailors have come *from* Avalon?' said Tusia.

'Because they get trapped,' ploughed on Smithies. 'We know the place they left behind is better than the place they land. When they're given the chance to go back to the place they've left behind, they choose to stay where they don't have to work and everything is "shadowy". It looks like they never return home to where they belong.'

He pointed to a section of the text for them to see.

'So this island they're on isn't really much fun?' said Sheldon, after he'd scanned the page.

'Not if you read the poem carefully. The sailors are being tricked. Nothing's real. After eating the lotos flower, they see a world that's not the best it could be. It's a shadow of what could exist. And does that remind you of any stories we've looked at before?'

'Plato's cave story!' blurted Brodie. Her heart was racing. 'You told me that story right at the start of this crazy adventure. People kept in caves and the only thing they saw were shadows projected on to the walls.'

'Well done, Brodie!'

The ideas were coming together like pieces of fabric in a patchwork. In Tennyson's poem, the sailors landed in a shadow world. A place where people didn't really see the truth.

'So d'you think the island in the poem's really any place that's not Avalon?' asked Sheldon. 'That the poem's reminding the Knights of Neustria they should just wake up and stop feeding on the lies they're being given? They should go back to a wonderful place where things are real. And *that* place is Avalon!'

'It could mean all that,' said Smithies. 'Oscar. You agree?'

Sicknote nodded vigorously.

'And you got all that from a poem about flowers?' said Kitty, plunging her hands deep into her pockets.

'It's what we do,' said Smithies. 'Dig deep to find answers. Go with ideas that could make sense.'

'And if you think about it, then it means unless we find Avalon we haven't really seen the world as it should be,' Brodie cut in. Her head was spinning, her palms burning. All these connections had to mean Avalon

Tennyson → The Lotus Eaters

Is a Lotus yummy?

Island
Not fantastic!

Plato → The Cave Story

Cave
^
Really a shadow world

Avalon → Is that the 'real world'?

wasn't only worth finding but it promised more than the life she knew.

Then something clicked and turned in her mind, as if she were trying to complete a jigsaw puzzle. She closed her eyes and concentrated hard, slotting the piece of puzzle into place. 'Oh, this is too crazy,' she said at last, jumping to her feet. She darted across the room and picked up another of the books of poems from the floor. 'This is one of my all-time favourite poems, and it's by Tennyson,' she said, sweat lifting like beads on her forehead. 'I don't know why I didn't think of it before, but it all fits in.'

'More islands?' urged Kitty.

'More shadows,' said Brodie, smiling at Smithies.

She passed around the poem book open on the page showing a picture of a woman with a large mirror hanging behind her. Brodie read aloud the words beside the picture:

> *And moving thro' a mirror clear*
> *That hangs before her all the year,*
> *Shadows of the world appear*

'Tennyson wrote about this Lady of Shalott. She lived in a tower away from everybody else.'

Sheldon put up his hand. 'Queen's Tower,' he said.

'That's the title of the third movement of Elgar's Arthur music. We should've realised there'd be a link to towers somehow in this enormous puzzle.'

Brodie's mind flitted back to the CD inlay Sheldon had shown them, her excitement growing.

'This lady,' cut in Tusia. 'She looks kind of sad.'

'She was,' said Brodie. 'She was very sad.'

'Why?'

'Because she could only look at the world through a mirror. She desperately wanted to look out at the world, but she wasn't allowed to.'

'Pretty miserable way to live,' said Hunter.

'Then one day, she heard something. And that's important, I think. It was the sound that did it. That detail confirms clues can be in things we hear.'

'Like Elgar's music,' pressed Sheldon.

Brodie nodded.

'So what did this lady hear, then?' asked Tusia.

'Lancelot outside the tower. And she couldn't bear not to look and so she did.'

'And what was so special about Lancelot?' said Tusia, hanging on her every word. 'I mean, apart from him being a knight in shining armour, which I totally object to because it sounds so sexist, as if the only thing girls are interested in is people who can fight.'

'No. That's the brilliance,' said Brodie, her heart

71

racing in her throat. 'I'd never thought of it before, but Lancelot was *more* than just a knight. He had this whole back story. You know – complicated past.'

'Ooh, I like those,' said Tusia. 'Dark secrets and all that. Makes people interesting.'

Brodie felt a little uncomfortable but she ploughed on. 'When he was tiny, Lancelot's dad, the King of Ban, was killed, because the castle they lived in caught fire. Lancelot's mum ran away. She put Lancelot, just for a moment, beside a lake and ran back to try and find her husband. She never came back though.'

'She died too, then?' asked Kitty. 'One dead parent. One missing. Not good.'

Brodie felt even more uncomfortable. 'So the Lady of the Lake came and took Lancelot somewhere special.'

'And I bet the last chocolate chip cookie I can guess where that place was.'

'Avalon,' Brodie said.

'Oh, yes,' yelped Hunter, punching the air. 'I am totally cooking on full gas today.'

'How does she know all this again?' asked Kitty, peering forward in an obvious attempt to take attention away from Hunter's rather unusual victory dance.

'It's her thing,' explained Tusia. 'The fact she's read every story ever written.'

'Oh, her happy ever after thing,' said Kitty.

The Lady of Shalott

Lived in a tall tower

Looked at the world through a mirror

Heard Lancelot

A knight whose dad died in a fire

↓

Left beside Lake

↓

Rescued by the lady of the Lake

↓

Taken to Avalon

Brodie wiped away a bead of sweat from above her eye.

Tusia took the poem book and pored over the picture. 'So this woman? This Lady of Shalott? She gave up looking at a world of shadows and reflections and she looked for Avalon. Is that what you're saying?'

Brodie nodded.

'And it finished well for her then, did it? Looking for Avalon. It was a happy ever after ending for her?' It was Hunter who posed the questions.

Brodie felt her stomach fall, as if she'd entered a fast-moving lift. 'Not exactly.'

'How come?'

Brodie took back the book of poems and turned the pages. She held the picture so they could all see. 'The lady escaped from the tower and sailed down the river.' She turned the final page.

In the last picture, the Lady of Shalott was clearly and most indisputably dead.

The Director paced in front of the pinboard.

'I'm sorry, sir.'

The Director did not break his stride. 'You're telling me there's nothing new, Wheeler. No progress at all?'

Wheeler clenched his hands into fists. 'No, sir. There's nothing. Seems there's not much discussion going on in the drawing room. They must have another place at Bletchley where they talk.'

The Director groaned. 'What good comes of talking anyway? We need action, Wheeler, and we need it fast.'

'Jaeger said in his letter to Elgar the thought of being without music and pictures and Sunshine made his heart feel *heavy, heavy as lead and tears flow readily*,' said Brodie as they negotiated their way past the spluttering water feature and towards their huts for bed. 'Do you think finding Avalon's worth the risk?' she said.

Hunter ran his fingers through his hair and shook off the water he'd been unable to avoid. 'We're always saying this is a risky business,' he said. 'Nothing's changed.'

'But if the Lady of Shalott had just been happy to keep watching the world in the mirror she wouldn't have died.'

'True,' said Sheldon. 'But didn't you say it yourself, it was the sounds she heard which made her turn?'

Brodie wrinkled her nose. 'I don't know what you mean.'

'We've heard the music of Avalon, Brodie. We can't read MS 408 yet. We don't know what the world will look like when we turn and face it. But we can't keep looking through a mirror. We have to work out what the unreadable writing says. And when we can do that,' he said, 'we'll see Avalon.' He linked his arm around her shoulder. 'For now, we just have the taster. The music drawing us in.'

'And suppose, if we turn to look at the source of the music, things end badly?'

'You're the "story girl",' Sheldon said softly. 'Are stories only worth reading if they end happily?'

Brodie swallowed. Then she shook her head.

'We've heard the music playing, Brodie, and we have to turn and see what we can see. That's what music does. It makes you look for more.' He took his harmonica from his pocket and pressed it to his lips and began to play.

'And so what do we do next?' Brodie asked.

'I think we follow the music down the river,' Hunter grinned.

'But what does that mean? What do we try and discover next?'

Hunter jumped in front of her and performed a quick jig in time to the music. 'There's a new plan,' he said. 'I heard Tusia and Smithies discussing it. We're leaving Bletchley for a while.'

6

The Tower on Fire

Kerrith looked down at her phone display. A single red light was flashing. She jabbed the screen with the stylus. The message was brief but that didn't matter. 'THE TEAM ARE ON THE MOVE. TRACKING IN PLACE.'

Kerrith slipped the stylus into the holder at the side of the phone. She turned off her computer then cleared her desk of papers.

Finally, she reached for her coat.

Fabyan handed a folded bank-note to the driver. 'Keep the change.' The driver checked the note, front and back, then stuffed it in his pocket before driving the taxi away.

Tandi stood at the end of the road, the mobile pressed tight against her ear. As Fabyan joined her she ended the call and slipped the phone back in her bag. 'They're leaving Bletchley. Following a lead,' she said. 'I've told them we've made progress. Explained we wanted to check things here before we go back to Station X.'

Piercefield House stood across the grass in front of them. Its walls crumbled, windows broken. It looked like no one had been near it for months. Except . . .

Fabyan bent down and pressed his hand on the grass. Dried tyre tracks running beyond the end of the road and towards the derelict building. He wiped his hands together. Dust flaked down to his boots. 'Let's find Mr Willer,' he said urgently.

'Why exactly have we come to London?' asked Brodie, tightening her Pembroke blazer around her as the wind whipped litter in spirals along the pavement.

'Death,' said Hunter.

'Excuse me?'

'Death. It's Sicknote's idea. Said checking out Tennyson's grave to see if we could find some extra clues was a really great idea.'

Sicknote hurried over to join them as they pushed their way through the hordes of tourists bustling outside

Westminster Abbey. 'Bacon's death-bed letter helped us, right? And think about how using the memorial stone at Piercefield and St Arvan's memorial tree made everything clearer. Graves can help that way. The most important thing you need to know about someone may be written on their grave. It's worth a look, don't you think?'

Brodie nodded. She was up for any exploring that made things clearer.

'OK,' said Smithies, drawing them all together as if they were in a rugby huddle. 'Keep close and try not to draw attention to yourselves. Merge with the tourists. Understand? We don't want any eyes from Level Five focusing in on us.' He passed a wad of cash along the line.

'Wow. We have to pay to get in,' said Hunter, staggering a little as he bounded up the stairs towards the sign at the entrance. 'Good job Fabyan's left us some money!'

'Here,' said Tusia, passing out some pamphlets. 'I've got us plans of the place.'

Brodie opened the leaflet but for a moment found it difficult to focus. The size of the abbey was overwhelming. She peered up at the vaulted ceiling and a shiver charged down her spine. 'This place is amazing,' she whispered.

'So,' said Hunter, breaking through Brodie's reverie, 'Tennyson's grave. Where will we find that?'

Tusia rolled her eyes and flapped the plan in the air. 'Erm, Poets' Corner,' she said. 'Surely the clue's in the name.'

'I was just testing,' he offered unconvincingly. 'What exactly is this Poets' Corner, then?'

'Lots of writers are buried there,' explained Sicknote. 'It's become a tradition.'

'Sort of cosy, then,' said Hunter as they made their way down the aisle to the South Transept. 'Them all being together.'

'Like a team,' grinned Brodie. Her skin prickled and her forehead burned.

'You OK, Brodie?' said Sicknote, recognising the signs of illness. 'Feeling faint; having a "turn"?'

'No. It's just . . .' She tried to make sense of what she felt. 'All these authors buried here. All these people who've given us the most incredible stories . . .'

'Calm down, B. It's not like they're family.'

Brodie didn't answer him. But she knew he was wrong. She made her way towards the stone commemorating Charles Dickens and then to Rudyard Kipling. Hunter just didn't understand.

They came to an opening at the end of the nave and Brodie looked down at the ground. Floor-stones butted together like a patchwork quilt.

'I've got the list,' said Tusia, pulling a piece of paper from her pocket. 'The four things we're looking for according to that letter to Elgar.' She read it again to remind them. '1. Green Fields 2. Quartets 3. Poetry 4. Pictures.'

'We're not looking for green fields in here, are we, Toots?'

'We could begin with pictures,' suggested Granddad. 'Loads of pictures in an abbey.'

'Not so many on a grave, though,' cut in Sicknote. 'People tend to go for angels or crosses or—'

'Firebirds!' cried Brodie.

'Well, I suppose it would be good for us if—'

'Look!' she hissed, dragging Granddad by the arm. 'What about that for a picture!'

'It can't be,' said Hunter. 'It's too obvious. Too clear. Too—'

'Too amazing,' chipped in Tusia, who'd darted across the stones and was bending down focusing on the raised image on the furthest grave. 'You can't tell me this is here by mistake.'

Brodie felt her throat tighten, her mouth dry. Tusia's hands were running across the image of a phoenix rising from flames. 'Unbelievable,' she whispered. 'Totally unbelievable.' She bent down beside Tusia to read more. '*D.H. Lawrence. Homo Sum! The Adventurer.*'

'What does that mean?' asked Kitty.

'*I am human*,' said Granddad. 'I understand what it is to be human.'

'And d'you think D.H. Lawrence has a phoenix on his grave because he was a Knight of Neustria?' whispered Brodie.

'Perhaps?' said Smithies.

'Over here,' yelped Tusia. 'Check out this picture! It's only a griffin!'

Brodie glanced over to where Tusia stood looking down at a large stone slab. Above the griffin marked near the base of the stone was a list of names. The stone explained those named were buried nearby.

'Chaucer,' gulped Brodie, scanning through the list. 'One of the most famous writers who ever lived. D'you think Chaucer was a Knight of Neustria?'

'His name's above a picture of a griffin,' said Smithies. 'It seems too clear a clue to ignore it.'

'And so it's just a branch that's missing,' said Hunter. 'We've got a phoenix and a griffin. Two of the three symbols of the Knights of Neustria. But there's no third symbol.'

'There's no branch,' Sheldon muttered. 'But look at this.' He bent down to point at another floor stone.

'Blossom. That grows on branches. And this blossom just happens to be *on fire*.'

This was just too spooky for words.

Sheldon traced the picture on the stone and then read the inscription aloud. '*The communication of the dead is tongued with fire beyond the language of the living.* Nice quote from T.S. Eliot,' he said.

Brodie pressed her hands together, trying hard to think. 'A phoenix and a griffin and blossom from a tree. What if they all lead here to a message from the Knights of Neustria?'

Granddad linked his arm around her. 'And maybe the message is, we have to listen to the words of the dead. That's what the writing on the floor stone says.'

'So, somewhere here, there really could be a message from Tennyson. It makes total sense. It has to be here,' urged Tusia.

'So let's find Tennyson's grave then,' encouraged Sheldon. He stood up and led them forward.

But Brodie felt herself buckle under a surging force of disappointment when they looked at the very next stone.

'It's Tennyson's,' said Hunter. But his voice was sad and hollow.

'This can't be all there is,' mumbled Tusia.

Brodie felt the coldness of the abbey wrap around

her. She could hear no whispers from Tennyson's grave. He was totally and utterly silent. There was no message about Avalon. Just his name, the date he came into the world and the date he left it. Absolutely nothing more.

'I take it this isn't what you hoped to find,' said Kitty, peering over Brodie's shoulder at Tennyson's memorial stone.

'That's the understatement of the year,' sighed Smithies, removing his glasses and rubbing them on his sleeve, hoping to make his vision so much clearer a missing clue would surface from the black marble.

'I can't believe it!' moaned Tusia. 'No cryptic clue, no inscription, no quote. Nothing. He was supposed to be all about the words. It just seemed so obvious there'd be something here, what with the pictures of the phoenix and the griffin and the flower. I mean, why have all those images if they weren't to help us find a hidden message?'

'Don't know, Toots. Maybe they're just a fluke. Although the probability of a phoenix, a griffin and blossom being the only images here is incredibly small.'

'But they're not the only images, are they?' said Tusia, stepping forward. 'I mean, there's *that* picture and that one makes no sense at all.' She pointed down at the floor stone for Gerard Manley Hopkins. Above his name and the words 'Immortal Diamond' a tower had been carved. Flames twisted from the windows. 'What is that? A tower? On fire?'

'Could be fire. Like the whole phoenix idea. And tongues of fire from the dead,' said Sicknote.

'Or it could be a tower like the one the Lady of Shalott lived in, filled with light and mirrors,' said Sheldon. 'That would link us back to Tennyson.'

Brodie was trying to take it all in. 'It's a fourth picture. The Elgar letter said we had to look for a quartet. Maybe this fourth image is important. A phoenix, a griffin, blossom and a tower. Maybe all four of them are connected to Knights of Neustria?'

'OK. Let's go with that idea,' said Smithies. 'Let's remember the tower. But it still doesn't make up for the lack of message on Tennyson's grave. Are we sure there's nothing else from Tennyson here?'

Brodie turned to walk back to Tennyson's gravestone. At the dark marble slab on the ground, she knelt down. 'Come on, Tennyson,' she whispered quietly. 'What are we supposed to see?'

As she traced the letters forming his name, her attention was caught by the light coloured slab on the ground beside Tennyson's stone. It was brown and cream marble and stood out against the black of Tennyson's. Brodie read the inscription.

ROBERT BROWNING MAY 7 1812 – DEC 12 1889.

'Weird, that,' said her granddad, who'd come to stand beside her.

'What's weird?'

'Well, the leaflet says both Tennyson and Browning were buried here and their wives were buried somewhere else.'

Brodie looked up. 'And Tennyson was buried *after* Browning?' she asked.

'A few years later, it says here. Why?'

'Well, Tennyson's buried next to poets, not his family. He's sandwiched between T.S. Eliot's stone, that tells us to listen hard to the language of the dead, and Browning's. I wonder if this Browning said anything important. Something which connects things together?'

'He was a writer, Brodie. He said a lot. How d'we know what could be the things we need to hear?'

'Well, I don't know. What was his most important work, for example?'

She took the leaflet from him and turned the pages.

'*Browning's most important work was considered to be THE BOOK AND THE RING.* That *has* to be important,' she yelped. 'The book and the ring. Don't you see? MS 408 and the ring worn by the Knights of

87

Neustria. It can't be a coincidence that of all the graves here, Tennyson's buried next to this one. Surely it's a sign we're on the right track.'

'You think all the graves here have a message connected to the Knights of Neustria?' asked Sicknote, who'd walked over to join them. He lowered his voice as a group of rather elderly women, wearing name badges and almost identical walking shoes, hurried past behind a tour group leader who was brandishing 'grave-rubbing paper' and charcoal pencils.

'I don't know,' whispered back Brodie. 'Maybe. Do you? Or perhaps the things around the graves.'

'Like those creepy head things?' said Sheldon.

Brodie peered at him.

'The statues,' he said, pointing.

Brodie turned to look at the busts around the walls. 'Well, is there one of Tennyson?' she urged, her excitement rising again.

Tusia scoured the space. 'Here,' she yelped. 'This is Tennyson.'

'Any messages?' pressed Brodie, racing over to join her.

'Nothing. No words at all.'

'Well, what about the other statues? Other Knights? Maybe we need to look for another three of them,' suggested Hunter.

'Why another three?'

'The quartet bit, B. We've found four pictures so maybe now we find four statues. Maybe to complete the quartet we have to find three more statues which do something more than Tennyson's cos that tells us nothing.'

'Statues of who?' implored Tusia.

'What about Coleridge?' offered Sheldon. 'He was the reason the Cambridge Apostles were set up. He's the person who made us think of Tennyson in the first place.'

'Well, yes, that'd be great,' said Brodie. 'If there's a statue of Coleridge then . . .' She stopped talking. The way Tusia was looking at her made the words dry in Brodie's mouth. 'Have you found a statue of Coleridge, Tusia?'

Tusia's only answer was a smile. She ran her hand around the tall pillar which supported the bust of Tennyson. On the back of the pillar was another statue head. Another bust. And the bust was of Samuel Taylor Coleridge. Perfect. 'You see,' giggled Tusia. 'It's like some giant puzzle and if we just put the pieces together we'll find the answer.'

Brodie tried to concentrate.

'OK, marble face,' joked Hunter. 'Let's have you rustle up your secrets like an "eat all you can" buffet. We're waiting.'

Brodie peered at the statue, half expecting it at any time to come to life, clamber down from its perch and tell them everything.

Nothing happened. They peered at the bust. The abbey grew colder. Just like Tennyson's grave, there were no words or texts. No hidden clues.

'We need to find two more,' said Hunter. 'Two more statues to complete the quartet.'

'But which two? There's loads of statues here.'

'*Next to*,' Tusia said quietly. 'It's important who Coleridge is *next to*. Like the graves.'

'OK, Toots. Who's Coleridge next to? Where's our clue?'

Tusia looked up. To the side of the bust was a statue of a standing man. 'Campbell,' she read quietly. 'Thomas Campbell. And if we're looking for clues then I think the words chosen for his memorial work well.'

Brodie read the words aloud.

> *'This spirit shall return to him,*
> *Who gave its heavenly spark,*
> *Yet think not sun, it shall be dim,*
> *When tho'u thyself art dark,*
> *No! It shall live again and shine,*
> *In bliss unknown to beams of thin*
> *By him recall'd to breath*

Who captive led captivity
Who robb'd the grave of victory
And took the sting from death.'

'Great quote about light and dark. I'm liking this Campbell guy,' said Hunter. 'What do we know about him?'

'He wrote a great poem, about getting old,' said Granddad. 'It was about a river. A river of life.'

'Like the river the Lady of Shalott sailed along in her quest for Avalon?' asked Sheldon.

'I guess,' said Granddad.

'So what's the message of the poem?' said Tusia, wrinkling her nose.

'It's to tell those with youth on their side to look around,' said Granddad. 'Before it's too late. I guess that fits with the Lady of Shalott looking round for the very first time as she sailed down the river from the tower.'

'Great,' said Hunter. 'I get it. We look around. But what at now?'

Brodie felt her face break into a smile. 'The memorial *next to* Coleridge on the other side, of course. The fourth part of the puzzle.'

She shuffled forward and as she did so, Hunter clutched her arm tightly.

'I think we've found the fourth part of the quartet,' whispered Sheldon.

Next to the Coleridge bust was a memorial of the most famous writer in the world.

Buried Alive

The Director looked at his watch. He was getting impatient. He hadn't heard from Kerrith. But at least she was on the move now. No, this didn't trouble him as much as the other lack of news. He opened the top drawer of his desk. The unrolled scrolls were as he'd left them. Laid out, one on top of the other, their black edges aligned.

He scanned the emblem in each corner of the uppermost scroll. The earth; the wind; the water; and the fire. Then he rested his finger on the monogrammed letter 'T'.

He still felt the same excitement he'd felt months ago on the day the first scroll arrived. It meant he was being watched. That his work to try and suppress the truth was noticed. He still knew little about the organisation that sent the scrolls. Only that they were in charge. Of everything. He knew they were tracking all he did.

And he also knew that however the organisation worked, he should have heard more by now.

It was taking too long.

'Brilliant!' said Tusia. 'We're back to the wheel.'

'The what?' said Kitty, her eyes widening.

'Cipher wheel,' said Tusia, obviously expecting this would be enough of an explanation.

'We had this monster contraption,' cut in Hunter, spreading his hands apart to give some sense of the size. 'We had to cut up books and stick them on the thing. Then we had to turn the wheel and read. It wasn't pretty,' he added.

'It certainly did the job, though,' said Sicknote. 'We found the hidden code written in *Morte D'Arthur*.'

'What's that got to do with Shakespeare?' asked Kitty, staring up at the statue.

'The cipher wheel was made to find messages hidden in Shakespeare's writing,' Brodie explained patiently. 'There were loads of codes in his work. We found one about the River Wye! So his monument being here is perfect!'

'And you think there may be codes in his statue?' said Kitty.

'Don't see why not.'

The group moved closer so they could see the memorial more clearly.

'Pretty impressive, don't you think?' whispered Tusia.

'Guess you'd like something like that, B, when you've toasted your last T cake?' joked Hunter, pointing at the part of the sculpture where Shakespeare was leaning his weight on a pile of books.

'It's nice, but I'm in no hurry to have a memorial, thanks. Are you trying to get rid of me or something?'

'No. I was just saying. All the books. It's a nice touch. Better than just his head peering out at us.'

Tusia glanced around at the other busts which ranged the walls. 'It's so different to the others,' she said. 'They've used the space to say so much. Must have been a really clever sculptor.'

'Well, according to the notes in the leaflet,' said Sheldon authoritatively, underlining the name with pen, 'it was some Flemish guy called Peter Scheemakers.'

'I've heard of him,' said Granddad. 'He did loads of work for that society I told you about. The Society of Dilettanti.'

'What? The group from Cambridge University?'

Mr Bray nodded.

'So come on then. Let's check this fourth statue for clues,' urged Hunter. 'Can't be a mistake we've been led to find old Shakey again!'

They peered in together. Shakespeare was pointing with his fingers on his left hand to words inscribed on a scroll.

Brodie read them aloud:

> '*The Gorgeous Palaces,*
> *The Solemn Temples,*
> *The Great Globe itself,*
> *Yea all which it Inherit,*
> *Shall Dissolve;*
> *And like the baseless Fabrick of a Vision*
> *Leave not a wreck behind.*'

'What does that mean?' said Kitty. 'Is it a clue?'

'It's from *The Tempest*,' explained Brodie. 'My favourite play. It's Prospero's line.'

'And who's Prospero, when he's at home?'

'A duke,' explained Sicknote. 'But he wasn't at home much.'

'Why? Where was he?' pressed Kitty.

'On an island! An island where he discovered magic!' Brodie could barely contain her excitement. Another island link. Of all the plays Shakespeare wrote, of all the poems and the sonnets. Of all the lines which could have been chosen, they'd discovered this one on his memorial. Spoken by a man who lived on a magical island.

'This can't be a coincidence, then?' said Tusia. 'I mean, it can't be, can it?'

Sheldon shook his head. 'We come here to look at the grave of Tennyson and it says nothing. Then we find a quartet of clues linked to words rising from the fire; a ring and a book; a river and an enchanted island. It's like everything's come together.'

'It can't be chance,' said Hunter. 'It all fits together like a well-made club sandwich.'

'Well, you're right. All the clues link together,' encouraged Smithies. 'But do they lead us somewhere new? Do they give us another clue to follow?'

Brodie opened her mouth to answer him, but her lips seemed to stop working.

'B? You OK? You know where we should go next?'

Brodie couldn't answer. She could only point.

She'd know her anywhere. The way she walked; the angle of her head; the flick of her hair as she laughed. She was laughing now, with the steward at the door. A mocking, condescending laugh as he offered her a leaflet.

Kerrith.

'How? When?' The questions came thickly and Brodie wasn't sure who was asking what. Only Kitty was silent. Kitty didn't understand.

'It doesn't matter why or how,' gulped Smithies. 'All that matters is that she's here and she mustn't see us.'

'Is she alone?' blurted Brodie.

'Can't tell!' said Hunter. 'How would we know?'

There were hundreds of people in the abbey. Any one of them could be working for Level Five, tracking their every move.

'So we can't leave,' hissed Tusia.

'What d'you mean?' How could staying around ever be a good idea when that woman was concerned! Things never ended well if she was near. Brodie's mind was beginning to swim. Tusia grabbed her arm and pulled her into the recess beside Shakespeare's statue.

'They could have people at the doors. If we leave, they'll see us.'

'So what d'we do?'

'We make ourselves invisible. Make her think we were never here.'

Brodie struggled to understand.

'We have to hide!'

It was a crazy idea. Everything inside Brodie wanted to run. To be outside in the air and away from this place. But Tusia was right. Kerrith wouldn't be alone. Making for the exit was not an option.

Tusia peered around the corner and flapped open the map. Poets' Corner was marked by a number 6. 'OK!' hissed Tusia. 'Somewhere quiet. Less obvious.'

Brodie could feel sweat beading on her forehead.

'It's the only way,' urged Tusia. 'You have to trust me!'

Brodie wasn't about to argue. Footsteps were echoing down the aisle. Any set of them could be Kerrith's. Any one of the tourists could be a worker from Level Five.

Tusia nodded. It was a silent clue. Brodie knew what it meant. Tusia was in charge.

Tusia led the way from Poets' Corner. Her steps were quick, but she didn't run. Nothing to draw attention to themselves. Brodie's heart thumped with every step. The bead of sweat ran down from her forehead and into her eye. Tusia kept walking.

They passed signs for the Chapter House. The crowd was thinning slightly. Brodie didn't look back. Tusia knew where she was taking them.

The sign said the Pyx Chamber was closed after 4 p.m. Brodie glanced at her Greenwich Mean Time watch. It was way past four. Tusia unclipped the fastening of the rope across the entrance and one by one they made for the stairs. When she re-clipped the sign, it swung a little in the breeze.

Tusia picked up the pace as they hurried down into the hidden part of the abbey. Their footsteps rang on the tiled floor and the air was colder now. There was less light.

The chamber had huge vaulted ceilings, thick columns in dusky stone. A huge altar at one end. The space was deathly quiet. And empty.

'Why are we—'

Sheldon cut Kitty off. He could hear. They all could. Footsteps on the stairs. They'd been followed.

There were no windows; no doors, just a space that echoed with every step. There was no other way out. Tusia had led them into a trap. This was it. No chance of escape.

'There!' ordered Tusia. She pointed at two huge rectangular boxes at the end of the chamber.

'You've got to be kidding—'

Tusia held up her hand. 'We've got no choice.'

She darted across the room and swung open the lid of the nearest box. It was empty. It stank of wood stain and copper and dust. Hunter hurried towards the second box. He swung open the lid. Brodie could hardly breathe.

She wasn't sure who climbed into which box. They helped each other as if they were scrambling into lifeboats but there was barely any space and the sides of the box dug into her arms.

'Here,' yelped Brodie, reaching for Sheldon's hand. He tumbled in beside her and as he grabbed her hand the leaflet he held fluttered free. Brodie's heart lurched. As the lid swung closed the paper rolled across the floor.

'It's marked,' she hissed. 'Scheemakers! You marked his name!'

'Brodie. Leave it! Please! It's too late!'

Brodie fought off his hand in the darkness. She pressed hard against the lid. It creaked open. She groped upwards as if digging herself free from her own grave. She crawled across the floor and grabbed the leaflet. She balled her hand into a fist and then lurched upwards again for the box.

The footsteps were louder. Nearer the bottom of the stairs. Seconds away.

Hands helped Brodie back into the box. The lid scraped against her shoulder, a loose nail ripping at her blazer. She stifled a gasp. Flung herself down in the space.

In the darkness under the closed lid it was impossible to tell who was beside her. She could feel breath on her skin, a rustle of clothing to her side. Tusia's hair maybe, against her throbbing shoulder.

Inside the box there was total darkness. No slits of light. Just black. Her eyes were useless. They stung with sweat. Her hand tightened on the map.

She could hear her own heart beating. Was sure that whoever was pacing now inside the chamber would hear it too. Footsteps getting louder. Getting closer. And then a voice. Kerrith's voice. 'You're sure they came down here?'

'Yes, ma'am.'

Brodie tried to swallow. Air clogged in her mouth. Her eyes stung and her knees dug hard into her chest.

'Then find them.'

Brodie closed her eyes and the darkness burned. A sound of a weight pressing down on the lid of the box. A hand perhaps.

No more footsteps. Silence. All she could hear was her own heart.

Tandi stood by the fireplace. The broken walls of Piercefield House strained up towards the sky. There was a line of washing hanging between the crumbling pillars. The washing was grubby. There were logs stacked in the corner. The grate was filled with only ash. There was a mug of tea balanced on an upturned crate. It had a skin of mould across it.

'He's not here,' Fabyan said reluctantly. 'Looks

like he hasn't been here for weeks.'

Tandi took the notebook from her bag and flicked to the page titled 'MISSING'. Under the names Evie and Miss Longman she added another name. Mr Willer.

'We need to get back to Station X,' she said.

Brodie heard new voices. Louder. Hurried.

This was it then. This was the end.

She screwed up her eyes and clenched her fists. And she tried not to breathe.

'I'm sorry. This chamber is closed to the general public.'

The lid of the box banged a little. A hand hurriedly pulled away.

'If you'd like to return tomorrow after ten I'd be happy to show—'

'That's quite all right. We've seen all we need to, thank you.' And that laugh again echoing on the stone floor.

Brodie wondered how long they waited there. Hidden in the boxes, scared to move. She guessed this was what being buried alive felt like. Suddenly she couldn't get enough air into her lungs. She pushed her empty hand against the lid. It lifted. Light flooded in. The chamber was empty. Kerrith was gone.

Brodie's nails from her closed hand had dug a line into her palm. When she opened her fingers to reveal the leaflet, there was a streak of blood across the crumpled page.

8

The House with
One Hundred Chimneys

'You have to stop!'

There'd been little discussion as they left the abbey. They needed to get away. And quickly.

Sicknote and Granddad were doing their best to keep up but Tusia, who'd been leading, was now suddenly behind them.

'Tusia, please!' insisted Smithies. 'We've had a close escape. Somehow Level Five are on to us. We have to make this right and get out of town. Now!'

No one had talked about how Kerrith had found them. Being in London was obviously not a good idea. Brodie tried not to think about how they'd been tracked to the abbey. They'd been so careful this time. But it seemed that every time they left Station X,

Level Five were close behind. Watching.

'Will you please just wait!'

Smithies stopped dead and the crocodile of people behind him spluttered to a halt.

'Look,' yelped Tusia, her voice high and strained.

'OK. We're looking. Busy London shoppers on their way to Chinatown,' said Brodie. 'And oh . . .' Her voice tailed away.

'You see it?' Tusia pressed.

'Oh, I see it!' said Brodie, her voice shaking a little. 'I see it all right!'

'Please, you two,' moaned Hunter. 'Do you have to do this every time? If you could just tell us what you see and . . .' He stopped speaking. He leant forward and peered in the direction they were looking.

'We haven't got time for this!' Sicknote looked a little green.

Brodie could see Tusia had on her 'I'm not going to take no for an answer' face.

Smithies looked across at Sicknote. 'Three minutes, Oscar. If Tusia thinks it's important.'

The green shadow darkened under Sicknote's eyes, but he nodded. 'Three minutes.'

Tusia turned and hurried through the crowds of people towards the middle of a large square.

'What part of London is this?' asked Sheldon.

'Leicester Square,' called back Kitty. 'I've been here before. But I've never really noticed him before.'

They slowed to a halt beside her and looked up.

'It's the same statue,' gasped Tusia. 'I mean, obviously not the *same* one, but, well, the *same* one,' she said again.

'Identical,' said Brodie. 'Bigger, but just the same as the one in the abbey. Same pose, same books, same scroll.'

Granddad stepped forward and pointed to the writing under the statue of Shakespeare. 'Nice,' he said slowly. 'This place was bought by someone called Albert Grant Esquire and given over to the people of London.'

Tusia wrinkled her nose. 'So why put a statue of Shakespeare on the top? Why not one of Albert Grant?'

Brodie was aware of a hot dog vendor standing close beside them. He was sniffing loudly, clearly keen for them to notice him. She shuffled awkwardly on the spot. 'That statue?' she said at last. 'D'you know anything about it? Or the man who put it there?'

The man pushed his Union flag hat higher up his head and put down the squeezy bottle of mustard he'd been refilling. 'That there's Shakespeare,' he said proudly.

'But what about Albert Grant?' asked Tusia.

''E was a typical MP,' sniffed the hot dog vendor. 'You know, always on the make. Lots of money scandals. Nothing changes.'

'But he gave this land to the people of London?' said Hunter.

The vendor nodded. 'Was a rubbish dump 'ere,' he said. 'Cleaned up the place since then, they have. Old Albert was keen on the arts and wanted people to have a park to enjoy. A green field to rest in.'

Brodie jabbed Kitty in the ribs. 'Green fields. On our list of four things mentioned in Jaeger's letter, remember!' Kitty nodded as Brodie turned again to the vendor. 'And this statue of Shakespeare is the same as the one in Westminster Abbey?' she said.

'Near as maybe,' he grinned. 'I mean, apart from the obvious.'

Brodie knew she looked confused.

'Well, the water round it for a start. No water in the abbey version.'

Brodie felt her skin prickle. A tingle in her arms.

'And there's the scroll, of course. The words on it. They're changed.'

Brodie could barely breathe 'thank you' as she hurried nearer to the statue. 'Well,' she yelped. 'What does it say?'

Tusia had clambered closest and called out the

words to those behind her. 'THERE IS NO DARKNESS BUT IGNORANCE.'

Brodie clutched tight to Hunter's arm. 'The sunshine,' she said. 'It's all about the sunshine and the light.' Her chest was burning with excitement. 'That line. The line about ignorance and darkness. It's from Shakespeare's play *Twelfth Night*.'

'How does she know all this?' asked Kitty.

Hunter winked. 'Chaos,' he said, 'BB knows everything!'

Brodie grinned. 'The clown says that line to Malvolio when everyone thinks Malvolio's mad.'

'And is he mad?'

'No,' said Smithies. 'They're trying to confuse him. He's in the dark and doesn't know what's going on.'

'So how does all this help us?' Kitty pressed.

Smithies strode up and down. 'Two statues of Shakespeare. One at a place where they bury people. One here at a place made beautiful after things were thrown away. Identical statues. Apart from the water at the bottom of this one which must mean water's important.'

'Water around an island, then?' said Tusia. 'Like the water here is making the statue into an island.'

'Exactly.'

'And the quotes?' added Sheldon. 'They're different, don't forget!'

Brodie twisted the end of her hair round her fingers. 'The quote in the abbey was from *The Tempest* and was all about death. But it comes from a section of the play where Shakespeare talks about the power of dreams. And here, with this statue, we're talking about the power of light to break through darkness. The power of light to overcome madness. It all fits with Jaeger's letter about Sunshine.'

'Brilliant, B,' grinned Hunter. 'Truly brilliant. But there's one thing you're forgetting.'

'There is?'

Hunter nodded his head. 'Numbers! You said the quote on this statue was from *Twelfth Night*. The number *twelve*. The perfect number, remember? And when did we think about that before?'

'When we talked about the Cambridge Apostles!' she blurted. 'When we decided there was twelve of them.'

'So now I think we have everything,' Hunter said. 'We have two statues where Shakey points to a message for us. One leads us to an island where dreams and magic are important. And one wants us to think about light and madness and the number twelve! This has to be important!'

'All that from two statues?' said Kitty.

'Yep. All that,' said Sheldon. 'Good this, isn't it? Glad you joined?'

Kitty looked a little awkward. 'I just don't know how you know what you're looking for. I mean, what things are important and what things aren't?' She tapped her foot against the ground. 'I mean, are these things clues?' she said.

'What things?' Brodie looked down. At Kitty's foot there was a small metal plaque sunk into the ground.

'Looks like some sort of distance calculator,' Mr Bray said, scanning the information. 'Showing how far places are away from here.' There was a sign for Malaysia and Singapore sunk into the ground to the left of where Kitty stood.

'Perhaps these markers are clues,' said Kitty defensively. 'Perhaps we need to travel to one of these places.'

Brodie looked down at the plaque nearest to her own feet directly in line with the outstretched arm of William Shakespeare.

The plaque read: FIJI 16275 KM

'My brothers are in Fiji,' said Tusia. 'Helping to save the planet.'

Brodie smiled. Tusia *had* mentioned that fact once

111

or twice during their night-time chats. 'It may be an important clue,' Brodie said, and she tried to hide the note of reticence from her voice. 'And we should definitely remember the details. Secret-breaking's all about the connections. So we'll remember.' She took the crumpled leaflet about the abbey and above the streak of blood across the back she jotted down the distance and the place.

'One six two seven five,' said Hunter, tapping the side of his head. 'Distance to Fiji. Consider it logged and recorded. Never forget numbers, me.'

Kitty looked impressed. And sort of grateful.

'Erm, three minutes,' cut in Sicknote, dabbing at his forehead with his sleeve. 'I really think we should move on.'

'Move on to what?' asked Tusia. 'What do we do with all this information? Where do we go now?'

No one was sure of an answer.

'Scheemakers,' said Smithies at last. 'I think he's the link we need to follow. If he made this statue *and* the one in the abbey, then maybe there's more. Maybe he left clues in other things he made. It's got to be worth thinking about.'

'The sculptor,' said Tusia, turning to face Brodie's granddad. 'Didn't you say you knew about other statues he'd made?'

'He made lots of statues for someone called Anson – the man who started the Society of Dilettanti I told you about, remember? The guy who went to Cambridge University, so that gives us a possible link to the Cambridge Apostles.'

'Anson's house then,' said Smithies as he led the way back across the square. 'We start at Anson's house, and the Scheemakers statues there.'

'Now, come along, Angelika,' insisted Kerrith, her arms folded tight across her as if she feared her body would become contaminated by the air around her. 'I've explained I know they came to London again. And when they come to London, we know they stay at the Carthorse.' She spat out this last word like a piece of meat gristle she was finding hard to chew. 'Although why anyone would want to stay in this forsaken hole's totally beyond me.' She flicked a speck of dust from her shoulder with vehement disgust.

The Polish chambermaid held tightly to the stack of towels she'd prepared for room 17. 'I not know anything,' she said, clutching the towels against her chest.

Kerrith was growing impatient. 'Now, we both know that's not true, Angelika.' She smiled awkwardly. 'You don't mind me calling you Angelika, do you? You see, once I've discovered someone's name and all the little details about them, it seems a shame not to use them.' She pressed her lips together in a thin snarl. 'It's incredible how much about a person one can learn,' she added, 'like how long it is until an immigration visa's up for renewal, for example.'

The Polish chambermaid's hands loosened and the towels tumbled to the floor.

'You see, I knew we'd get there eventually. With a little reminder.'

Angelika fumbled on the floor for the towels.

'Just tell me,' Kerrith added. 'Are the team due back here tonight?'

Angelika shook her head.

'So they're going back to Bletchley, then. So soon?' Kerrith didn't hide the note of surprise from her voice. She clicked her heels together. 'Well. Is that where they're going?'

Angelica didn't answer.

'I've heard deportation can be a painful experience,' she said at last. 'If paperwork is found not to be in order. If, for example, it's been tampered with.'

Some of the towels were wrapped around Angelika's arms like handcuffs. 'They not go home,' she said eventually. 'They not stay in London but they not go home.'

'You see,' Kerrith sneered. 'That wasn't so very difficult, was it?' And turning to leave the hotel, Kerrith ground the heel of her shoe into the remaining towel on the floor at Angelika's feet.

Tandi pressed open the door of the Listening Post with her shoulder, then put down two cups of coffee on the windowsill. 'Any luck?'

Fabyan's answer came from behind a jumble of wires and cables. 'Nearly.'

Tandi grinned. 'Seriously. You want me to help with that?'

Fabyan held up two blue cables. 'I just can't seem to . . .'

'Here. Let me.'

It took about forty minutes but eventually Tandi took a seat in the swivel chair by the window and gulped down the dregs of her long-cold coffee. 'Think it will work?'

'I think it's cost a fortune and I don't think for a minute we'll be able to pick anything up. I can't imagine the Black Chamber's security will really let us piggyback on the remote connection but now we have the password it's worth a try. But I don't think we should get our hopes up and—'

The screen on the computer monitor flashed.

'Oh, I don't know,' said Tandi. 'Looks like we might just be in business after all.'

It was dark.

Sheldon had ridden with Kitty on the back of her motorbike. The rest were huddled inside the Matroyska. Tusia and Granddad were dozing and Sicknote was listening to a tape of meditation exercises.

Brodie moved closer to Hunter so she could whisper. 'D'you think he was in the abbey?' In the flickering light of the speeding traffic it was easy to see Hunter was confused. 'Friedman, I mean?'

'You think he was with them? With Kerrith and the rest from Level Five?'

'I don't know. Do you?'

Hunter turned to look out of the window. Brodie guessed he was scared to answer.

'If he isn't with them, if he hasn't changed sides, then why won't he come back?'

'This is so frustrating!'

Fabyan was at the window peering out into the darkness across the grounds of Station X. He turned and smiled meekly at Tandi. 'You've been at it for hours. Maybe it's time you took a break?'

Tandi ran the cursor across a line of files. It hovered

for a moment over one named KM but she didn't open it. Instead she leant back on her chair and took her hand off the mouse. 'I can't. It's impossible to work out how to get further into the system. The password just lets me into these personnel files, old reports, but nothing new. Everything else is password protected at another entry level. There must be a way round this.'

'Well, if there's a way I'm sure you'll find it.'

Tandi shrugged. 'Want a go?'

'I bought the equipment, Tandi. That's my contribution.'

'Technology not really your thing, then?'

'Hardly. Old stuff. Weird stuff, that's my thing. Thought you'd have worked that out by now.'

'And your wife? She didn't go along with all that, then?'

Fabyan turned back to the window. 'I thought she did.'

Tandi drummed her fingers across the computer keyboard.

Fabyan sighed. 'Maybe life was just not exciting enough for her. I don't know. She left a note. Said she'd had enough. That was it.'

'And you've not heard from her since?'

Fabyan didn't answer.

'I'm sorry.'

'Hey. Bad stuff happens.' He hesitated. 'So you going to show me these personnel files, then? They may lead us somewhere.'

'They might.' But Tandi wasn't really convinced.

'Surprise!'

Brodie took her hands down from her face and blinked.

'Well. What d'you think, B? Great, eh? Considering the restrictions of not being at home, I mean.'

A rather plump-looking woman, standing beside a long kitchen table strewn with streamers and surrounded by balloons, smiled broadly as Hunter waved appreciatively at her. 'Best guest-house in Great Haywood, don't you think? And best landlady?' He winked and the plump woman blushed right to the roots of her hair.

'This is all for me?' exclaimed Brodie, looking at the table which practically groaned under the weight of the fully cooked breakfast.

'The balloons and pressies are,' clarified Hunter, 'but you have to share the fry-up.' There was a note of almost desperate pleading in his voice. 'Happy Birthday!'

Brodie could hardly speak. She'd had no idea her

friends had remembered and had never in her life had a surprise party, let alone a breakfast party.

'So come on,' urged Hunter. 'Before it all gets cold.' He grabbed for a rasher of bacon. 'What?' he yelped, as Tusia poked him firmly in the ribs. 'She knows it's to share and I'm starving. It was your idea to let her sleep in. But now she's up, we need to get a move on. And,' he said, loosening a section of bacon caught in his teeth, 'don't get all defensive about the food. There's porridge and eggs for you. Mrs Hummel knows about your aversion to eating meat.'

'It's not an aversion,' began Tusia, drawing herself up tall beside Hunter. 'It's a political and moral decision that—'

'Guys,' said Brodie, pushing her way between them. 'It's my birthday. Any chance of you two being nice to each other?'

Tusia looked a little guilty, but Hunter simply made the most of her lack of attention to grab another rasher of bacon.

The meal was wonderful and afterwards Brodie sat with a contented feeling in her heart as well as her stomach.

'Now, we couldn't go to town with the gifts,' said Sheldon apologetically. 'Because the truth is, we couldn't go to town.' He laughed at his own play on words and Brodie humoured him with a smile. 'We had a quick trip to the village shop and so your pressies have a local theme.'

'Anything you've got me will be lovely,' she giggled.

'Seriously, B? Cos I was running low on cash,' Hunter said, passing her an open bar of Dairy Milk chocolate. 'And it was a really long walk back from the shop.'

Brodie smiled appreciatively, amazed he'd actually managed to save her half.

'We clubbed together,' said Tusia and Sheldon, passing a gift wrapped in a paper bag.

Brodie recognised the shape and weight of the package. She only hoped, as the present was handed over, it contained a book she hadn't read. She was running low on supplies.

She ripped at the paper to reveal, as expected, a book. *The Book of Lost Tales* by J.R.R. Tolkien. Sticking out from the page was a hand-drawn bookmark from Tusia. It was holding a page about Gilfanon's house in Tol Eressëa. 'The lady in the shop explained the story mentions a house with a hundred chimneys,' said Tusia. 'It's based on Shugborough Hall. That's Anson's house. The reason we're here. Tolkien saw the house while he was on holiday, and decided to write about it in one of his tales.'

'One of the best writers ever stayed nearby?' Brodie asked, excitement fizzing in her stomach.

'Tolkien actually stayed in this very house,' said Mrs Hummel as she hurried off into the kitchen.

Brodie hugged the book against her. 'Oh, this is brilliant,' she said. 'Absolutely brilliant,'

'My turn,' said Kitty, handing over a fairly bulky package which Brodie quickly discovered was thick leather gloves. 'These'll come in useful if you ever decide to ride pillion on my bike, you know. The man in the local garage was very helpful.'

Brodie felt herself turning a little green. She couldn't really see herself ever wanting to ride on the back of the bike.

'Here,' said Sicknote. 'Fabyan and Tandi chipped in too. Guessed it was time you had one. It's really for us all to keep in touch. Sent it special delivery and it arrived this morning.'

Brodie thanked him as he passed her a small box containing a mobile phone. 'Perfect!' she smiled.

Smithies moved forward next. 'From me and Mrs Smithies. Hoped it might be useful while we're travelling.' His package contained a small hand-mirror edged with intricate silver roses.

'Thank you,' she smiled, as he shuffled free of her hug.

'And here's another book to complete the set,' said Granddad. 'It's not my main pressie. That I'll give you later.' He seemed a little nervous. 'But this could be just what you need right now.'

'Very clever,' said Brodie, holding the book for them all to see. 'A history of Shugborough Hall. I can't think of anything we need more.'

'Well, how about a personal tour guide for the place?' said Tusia. 'You can't get everything you need from books. The personal touch adds the details.'

Brodie frowned. 'Well of course, a guide who could take us round and give us all the inside gossip would be great,' she said.

'Good job we've found one, then,' said Smithies.

'Yeah,' said Hunter, rubbing his overstuffed belly. 'Seems Mrs Hummel's not only the very best bed and breakfast host in Great Haywood, but she also works as a guide at the stately home up the road. And she's agreed to take us.'

'And will it be, you know,' Brodie hesitated a little as she searched for the right words, 'safe to involve her? It won't make her a target for Kerrith's people?'

'We've thought of that one,' Sheldon said. 'Smithies explained we're doing research in the hope of putting together some children's TV show about the place in the future. And that rival channels are after our ideas.'

He pushed his chest out proudly. 'We've made her swear not to breathe a word of our visit to anyone. And anyway,' he added confidently, 'no one will have the foggiest idea we've been here. We've been extra careful this time.'

Capture of the Treasure Ship

'Staffordshire,' snapped Kerrith. 'What on earth are they doing in Staffordshire? In fact, what would anyone want to do in Staffordshire? Isn't it just full of sheep and fields and pretty china?'

The man at the other side of his desk winced a little. 'Well?'

'The tracking device on the bike locates them in a village called Great Haywood, ma'am. We are, as yet, totally unclear about why they're there. But . . .' He hesitated. 'We note it's the girl's birthday.'

Kerrith sniffed with distaste. 'And?'

'Perhaps getting away is a sort of treat. Perhaps she's got family there.'

'You really need to pay attention, Wheeler.' Kerrith

wasn't amused. 'The whole point about this girl is her lack of family. Apart from her doddery old granddad, the kid has no one. That's the beauty of it all.'

Smithies was standing in the hallway of the bed and breakfast. Mrs Hummel had said it was fine to use the phone to ring his wife whenever he needed as long as he noted his calls.

'Sarah OK?' Sicknote asked.

Smithies' answer was non-committal.

'We'll be home soon. You mustn't worry.'

Smithies checked his watch and added the length of the call to the list by the phone.

'I've been meaning to ask you,' said Sicknote. 'How's the reading going? On Avalon?'

'Good,' said Smithies. 'It's making more sense. Becoming clearer.'

'And when will you explain all this to the kids?'

'When they're ready. At the moment I want them to concentrate on the code. They're doing well.'

Sicknote laughed. 'They're doing brilliantly. All of them. I can't quite believe how well they work.'

'It's why we used them, Oscar. Friedman and I knew kids would be the answer.'

Sicknote looked a little awkward. 'The kids have stopped talking about him, you know.'

125

'Can't blame them. Brodie keeps ringing – and nothing. Not a word from him. I can't believe he's really joined Level Five.'

'Can't believe? Or won't believe?'

'He was . . . is . . . a good man, Oscar. I really believe that.'

'Maybe for some people it's just impossible to be good.'

Smithies sighed. 'I think you'd better take a look at the stuff I've been reading about Avalon.'

Kitty rode behind on her motorbike. Hunter borrowed Brodie's new leather gloves and clung tightly to Kitty's waist, riding pillion. The rest of the team sang all the time as the Matroyska made its way from Great Haywood to Shugborough Hall. Sheldon managed to work into every song some reference to it being Brodie's birthday as Smithies handed round his supply of Jammie Dodgers for everyone in the Matroyska to share. Brodie was sure Hunter would be sad to miss the biscuits, so she shoved a couple in her pocket to give him later. She couldn't remember being happier for a very long time.

As they clambered down from the van, a light February drizzle was beginning to fall and so Mrs Hummel led them straight into the hall itself. 'We'll start in the library. I know you're interested in the sculptures here but it's best to get some sort of handle on who the Ansons were before we begin properly,' she explained. The light danced around the room, bouncing off mirrors on the ends of the shelves and making them appear to stretch on without end. The room was perfect. Brodie tried hard to concentrate.

'So,' said Mrs Hummel, obviously eager to get on with the tour. 'This home was bought by the Anson family in the seventeenth century. George Anson was Admiral of the Fleet in the Royal Navy during the early 1700s. He's famous for sailing round the world, and becoming the First Lord of the Admiralty.'

'Sounds important,' said Sheldon.

'Oh, he was. And he was brave and fearless on the seas.' She spoke as if she was talking about a personal friend, not someone who'd been dead for several centuries. 'One of his most impressive victories was when he defeated a Spanish galleon called *Nuestra Señora de la Covadonga*. It was full of all sorts of gold and riches. What he took from that ship changed his life forever.'

'What do you mean?' asked Brodie.

'Anson caught up with the *Covadonga* off Cape Espiritu Santo on 20th June 1743. But he'd been desperate to track it down. He'd lost lots of other ships in his fleet during the journey but nothing would stop him finding the *Covadonga*.'

'Because of the treasure?' asked Hunter.

Mrs Hummel nodded but she didn't seem committed to her answer. 'There was an awful lot of treasure! It made Lord Anson rich for life and gave his heirs and his brother enough money to build this amazing estate. But I'd always thought there was more to it than that somehow. It was an obsession for him, catching that ship. Despite all the dangers, he just wouldn't give up.'

Hunter threw Brodie a wink. They knew all about following something despite the dangers.

'Would you like to see the dining room?' Mrs Hummel said, sensing the mounting excitement in the room. 'I know you're keen to see the work of Scheemakers, and the first of his four sculptures at Shugborough is in this room.'

'Four!' blurted Hunter.

Mrs Hummel looked taken aback. 'Yes, four. We call them his quartet of works.'

Brodie saw Hunter's expression change.

'You all right, dear?' said Mrs Hummel. 'I did wonder if you should've eaten quite so much breakfast.'

Hunter shook his head. 'I'm fine. Seriously. More than fine. Let's see Scheemakers' quartet!'

* * *

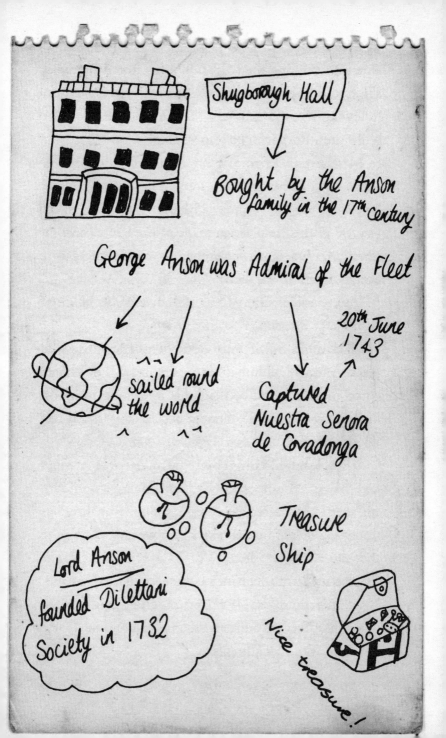

'Are you thinking what I'm thinking?' hissed Brodie as she hurried next to Hunter, down an ornate hallway, following Mrs Hummel's determined lead. 'Four sculptures. It's got to be important.'

Mrs Hummel's voice came from the dining room. 'Ahh. Good. Thought for a minute I'd lost you. Now, especially for the birthday girl who showed such an interest in the use Tolkien made of the house, here's a question. Do you remember how Tolkien used Shugborough in his work?'

'As an idea for a story about the house with a hundred chimneys,' Brodie said keenly.

'Well done. So chimneys are a bit of a feature of the place. And with chimneys come fireplaces. They rarely come more impressive than this one.' She moved a little across the room, standing back so they could see. 'Here's the first of the Scheemakers quartet.'

It was lovely. Marble covered with garlands of vines and masks. Brodie ran her hand along its smooth surface. It felt strangely warm, though the fire was unlit. 'Come on, Scheemakers,' she whispered. 'You're the reason we came here. Where's your message in the fireplace?' She ran her hands across each twisted garland. No words, no signs. No fingers pointing to important words like the sculptures had done in London. It was beautiful. But just a fireplace.

'The surround was added later than most things in this room,' explained Mrs. Hummel. 'All part of a restoration project. With so many chimneys belching smoke in the air, it was a good idea to make them beautiful.'

Tusia raised her head, as if watching invisible smoke drift from the fire. 'Look at the ceiling,' she whispered to Brodie from her position with her hand still resting on the fireplace. 'It could be a sign.'

'Why?' urged Brodie.

'The smoke from the fire would rise upwards, right? Point to the ceiling, like the finger on the Shakespeare sculptures pointed to the stories we needed to think about.'

'You think the story we need's up there?' said Brodie.

'Mrs Hummel,' said Tusia suddenly. 'That painting. On the ceiling. Is there a story behind it?'

'Oh yes. The painting shows "Apollo and the hours preceded by Aurora".'

'And what does that mean?'

'Apollo is the God of light and truth and music and poetry,' said Mrs Hummel.

Tusia dug Brodie firmly in the ribs.

'And Aurora? What's she all about?'

'She's the goddess of the dawn, who announces the arrival of light and the absence of darkness.'

Brodie felt a surge of adrenaline. This was turning into the best birthday ever. That was a connection, surely. All those references to light and sunshine. But they had to be careful. Not be certain about too much, too soon. She stood up. 'It's lovely, Mrs Hummel.'

'Glad you like it, dear,' the woman replied. 'But it's not my favourite of the quartet. To be honest, we've barely even begun. I think perhaps now the rain's eased, you'd best make the most of a chance to see outside in the grounds. The Ansons certainly had some interesting ideas about architecture out in the green fields of the estate.'

The use of the words 'green fields' made Brodie's heart press hard against her chest. The text of Jaeger's letter, with the cryptic instructions about where to look for clues, pulsed through her mind. Green fields. He'd said that. He'd made it clear. This really was turning into quite a birthday.

'A triumphal arch?' asked Sheldon as they hurried across the Shugborough estate, through the fields and as far away from the main house as it seemed possible to walk. 'What's one of them?'

Mrs Hummel looked over her shoulder as she led the way. 'The arch is all part of the work done in the late 1700s. The Ansons helped form the Society of Dilettanti,' she added.

'We've heard of it,' cut in Hunter.

'And the Society was interested in bringing building ideas from abroad to England.'

'And they brought an arch?' asked Sheldon, his forehead wrinkled in confusion.

'Not exactly. But they brought the idea for one.' Mrs Hummel slowed the pace a little. Then she pointed through the trees ahead of them.

Brodie gasped at the imposing structure. She shaded her eyes against the strengthening sun. 'That's incredible.' She waited for a moment, searching the stories in her mind for an explanation. 'It looks like a doorway with no door.'

'Like the entrance between two worlds,' added Tusia, leading the way towards it.

Brodie felt herself bristle with excitement.

'Except the world beyond the arch is just the same as the one this side,' Tusia called back, rushing under the archway, her arms stretched wide as she moved.

An image of a portal between earth and a land like Narnia thinned in Brodie's mind like smoke and drifted away, as Tusia reappeared unchanged. Her friend hadn't disappeared into a fantasy world – just stepped through to another part of the world that had always been there.

'The arch is a copy of the Arch of Hadrian in Athens. But it's also home to the second and third sculpture in the Scheemakers quartet. Look up there.' Mrs Hummel pointed skywards.

Brodie peered at the top of the arch more closely.

'There's sculptures two and three – the busts of Lord and Lady Anson. Either side of that "aplustre",' Mrs Hummel explained.

Brodie looked across at Granddad for a definition of the word 'aplustre' and he didn't disappoint. 'It's an ornamental structure rising up on a ship,' he said confidently. 'Something decorative which the flag of the ship is often attached to.'

Brodie took it all in. An arch looking as if it straddled two parts of the same world, and the decorative front of a ship, as if it was sailing from one to the other. It was brilliant.

Mrs Hummel seemed to register her concentration. 'You like it?' she said.

Brodie nodded.

'Well, in that case you'll want to see Scheemakers' most fascinating work here at Shugborough. His fourth sculpture. Follow me.'

* * *

Scheemakers
Quartet
(1-3)

① Fireplace

Triumphal
Arch

Sculpture
Lord A.
②

Sculpture
Lady A.
③

'What's that?' said Brodie as they walked back towards the main house building.

Mrs Hummel broke her stride. 'Oh,' she said, obviously a little distracted. 'Just a tower.'

Tower. Like the Queen's Tower in the Elgar music? Like the Lady of Shalott's tower? 'Is this what you wanted to show us?' Brodie said hopefully.

Mrs Hummel shook her head. 'What I want to show you is quite close to the mansion. But we can have a look at the tower if you're interested.'

'Yes, please. If that's OK?'

'What you doing, B?' hissed Hunter, running to walk alongside her. 'She was going to show us another Scheemakers sculpture. Why d'you want to go looking at a tower?'

Brodie found it difficult to answer. She wasn't really sure why. 'Because of the picture on the gravestone in Westminster Abbey?' she whispered.

'What? The tower on fire?' said Sheldon. 'You think this tower's on fire?'

Brodie frowned. 'Of course not. I just want to see it. Have a closer look. It's on the way to whatever Mrs Hummel wants to show us anyway.'

'Bet she's obsessing about some story. *Rapunzel* probably,' suggested Tusia knowingly. 'We may as well take a peek.'

Brodie smiled in appreciation and Mrs Hummel, recognising most of the group were keen to see it, led them forward.

It was an octagonal building with two arched doorways and a strange tubular mini tower attached to the side.

'I love the shape of it,' said Tusia. 'Totally bonkers. Do people go inside?'

'Of course,' said Mrs Hummel. 'I can show you.'

Brodie was the first to follow her in, but Tusia wasn't far behind, her smile widening as she gazed up at the intricately patterned ceiling.

There was an eerie quiet, a sort of hint of expectation. A breeze whistled through the air.

'I've just got a feeling this place is important,' whispered Brodie, masking her words with the back of her hand.

'I don't know,' Sheldon said sympathetically. 'It's nice and everything. But there's no pictures, no writings, no clues. And I don't think it's got anything to do with Scheemakers.'

'I think it's just a tower,' said Kitty.

Brodie felt the breeze against her face. She didn't know how she knew it, or why, but she was absolutely certain they were wrong.

Mrs Hummel led the way out. The sun was casting

shadows on the walls. 'Now,' she said confidently. 'If you follow me I'll show you what many people claim is Scheemakers' most important work.'

Brodie felt her frustration dissolve a little.

'Let me show you the Shepherd's Monument.'

Kerrith stood back from the notice-board. She was balancing a yellow-headed pin on her finger. The point was incredibly sharp.

'They're just obsessing with dead people,' said Wheeler, directing his gaze to the tapestry of notes attached to the board. 'It's not making any more sense.'

'And does any of this connect to the notes we took from Friedman's flat?' said Kerrith, pointing to a second board.

Wheeler shook his head. 'If it does, then I can't see the links.' He looked down at his shoes.

'The Director says we keep watching. We do nothing else.' Kerrith was not particularly happy about this part of the plan. She took the yellow pin and pushed it firmly into the second board. It skewered through a photograph of Friedman's face. 'Those irritants' obsession with the dead must lead us somewhere. Eventually.'

Secret of the
Shepherd's Monument

Mrs Hummel led the way to the north side of the grounds. The sky was darkening to an inky blue again and the air sparked with drizzle. The team didn't talk as they moved.

Finally, Mrs Hummel led them to a large stone archway, flanked by two thick stone pillars. Stretched across the top of the pillars was an ornate plinth. In the centre of the archway was a sculpted picture. It showed four stooped people, who looked a bit like shepherds, looking down.

Brodie stepped forward for a closer look.

The four figures were looking at a tomb covered with flowers and branches. On top of the tomb was a small pyramid. Across the tomb, letters were carved,

and two of the sculpted people were pointing at these letters although Brodie couldn't make out the words they formed.

Everyone was quiet. Brodie felt like she did in Westminster Abbey: cold and a little afraid. But this time there wasn't the excitement of being where great writers and poets had come for their final rest. This tomb was anonymous. It had no name she could make sense of.

'Whose monument is this?' Smithies asked at last.

Mrs Hummel laughed as if he'd made some

incredibly funny joke. 'We don't know,' she said at last.

'So why'd anyone go to the trouble of putting up a tomb or memorial for someone and not recording who it's for?' Hunter said.

'Oh, I understand your question and believe me, we've struggled with it too. All we know is this.' Mrs Hummel prepared to count off the facts she'd learnt as part of her training to be a guide. 'The monument was unveiled some time before 1758. Thomas Anson, George Anson's brother, asked for it to be built. Peter Scheemakers did the sculpted work. And the scene's actually a copy of a very famous painting by Poussin. You can see the title carved here on the tomb. The painting's called "Et in Arcadia Ego".'

'"Even in Arcadia I exist",' said Sicknote, wiping the increasing rain from the end of his nose. 'That's what it means. "Et in Arcadia Ego."'

'What exists?' asked Brodie.

'Death,' said Sicknote, his voice low and clear.

Mrs Hummel allowed them all to move nearer. She stood back a little, pleased they were so intrigued.

'So where's Arcadia?' whispered Sheldon.

'Lots of answers to that question,' said Sicknote. 'Most think it means a perfect place. A sort of paradise.'

'Could that perfect place be Avalon?' whispered Brodie. 'If the monument's connected to the secrets of the Knights of Neustria, then there's a chance, isn't there?'

'I suppose,' cut in Smithies. 'The stories about Avalon make it sound sort of perfect. Magic weapons and things.'

'So what does the picture mean, if it's trying to say something about Avalon here?'

Smithies tried to keep his voice down. 'If the shepherds are gathered round a tomb, maybe it means that even in a perfect place like Avalon, there's death.'

'Cheery thought,' grimaced Hunter.

'No. I think it's good,' Sicknote encouraged. 'If you think about it, maybe the picture's trying to help us see Avalon's real, not a fantasy place just from stories.'

Mrs Hummel was getting restless. The continual whispering was obviously unnerving her.

'And you really don't know who the monument's for?' said Tusia, sensing the need to draw their guide back into the conversation.

'It's not that we haven't tried to find out,' said Mrs Hummel. 'We've looked at all the Anson writings and we've tried to narrow it down.'

'Anson writings?' asked Brodie.

'Letters and diaries. I found some things I thought might be important. Words underlined in letters written by Lady Anson as if she was trying to draw attention to something.' Mrs Hummel searched through her bag. 'Three things Lady Anson underlined. I don't know why. But here.' She passed a notebook to Brodie. Three phrases had been written out.

With gold and silk

Fountain of True Love

Mirror of True Recognition

The phrases meant nothing to Brodie. 'This is great and everything but did Lady Anson write anything specific about the monument?'

'Lady Anson didn't. But there were poems. Two of them.'

'D'you remember them?' Hunter said hopefully.

'The first one's really long,' explained Mrs Hummel. 'By the writer Anna Seward. It was all about a hermit but it mentions the Shepherd's Monument because it goes on about *beauteous Marble moralizing the scene*. That must mean the picture on the front, you see. I remember bits of the verse.' She cleared her throat and began to recite.

> '*The silent monk, in lonely cell immured,*
> *From every folly, vice and care secured,*
> *Should inward turn calm Meditations Eye,*
> *And Life imploy in studying how to die . . .*
> *Through Fancy's flatterine glass he fondly views,*
> *That world, those joys he must for ever lose.*'

'Nice,' said Brodie, who'd absolutely no idea how the poem could help them.

'There was another one,' Mrs Hummel announced. 'We don't know who wrote that. But it talks about the monument again. Would you like to hear a bit?'

Everyone nodded.

> '*Let not the Muse inquisitive presume*
> *With rash interpretation to disclose*
> *The mystic ciphers that conceal her name.*'

'Ciphers!' pressed Tusia. 'As in codes?'

'Well, yes of course,' said Mrs Hummel. 'If you look closely at the bottom of the picture sculpted on the tomb, you'll see there's a cipher.'

Brodie stared at the base of the sculpted frieze.

'So this is a name, then?' suggested Hunter, peering closer too. 'The name of the person who the tomb was for, but it's been written in code?'

144

'Maybe,' said Mrs Hummel. 'Certainly the letters D and M mean *Dis Manibus* and they were often placed on Roman tombs. But the other letters are more confusing.' She hesitated. 'Perhaps it's a name. But I think there's too many letters for that. It's more likely to be some sort of secret message. Perhaps an acrostic with every letter being the beginning of a word. They were really popular at the time the monument was built. Used for hiding secrets.'

Brodie remembered making acrostics at school. It was a task a supply teacher often set the class. 'Write an acrostic of Christmas, or Fireworks or even your name,' they'd say. She could even remember one she'd written for her name.

B rave
R eader
O rganises
D ouble length
I ndividual
E nglish lesson

From what she could remember, the supply teacher hadn't been impressed.

'It's likely the acrostic's in Latin,' went on Mrs Hummel. 'That was used on religious memorials then. One suggestion is *Orator Ut Omnia Sunt Vanitas Ait*

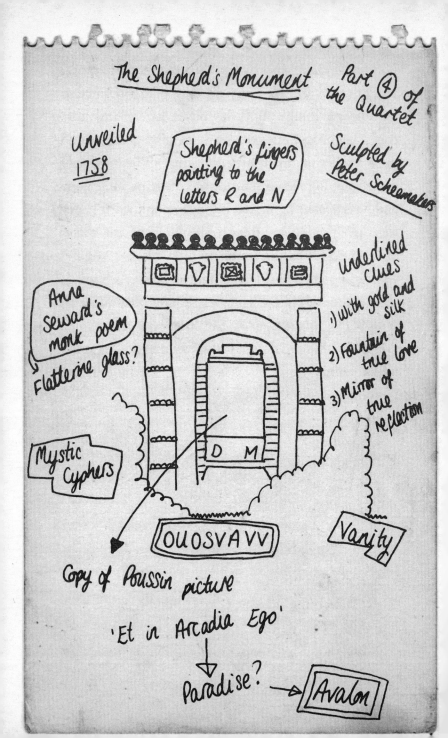

Vanitas Vanitatem, a version of the phrase *Vanity of vanities, saith the preacher, all is vanity*. It's supposed to be from the Bible . . . but it isn't an exact translation. And most people can't work out why *that* phrase would be there. Personally, I think the letters are a clue about something important connected to the Anson family and whoever the memorial is for.' She linked her hands together. 'So. Do you think you'll have enough, then?'

'Enough?' said Smithies, pulling his coat tighter around his shoulders.

'For your television programme?' said Mrs Hummel. 'I hope I've shown you lots to get you going?'

Brodie was too excited to form an answer. Her mind was scrambling over the letters from the monument, trying desperately to find a message hidden by the details:

O U O S V A V V

O bviously
U ncle
O scar
S earched
V ery
A nxiously
For **V** eronica's
V iolin

She smiled. It was a start. But she wasn't even sure this would impress a supply teacher, and she was absolutely certain it wasn't the answer to the code on the Shepherd's Monument.

'What do you mean, there's been a breach of security? Is this anything to do with the D notice on MS 408?' Kerrith choked back her anger. 'How could this have happened? How could you have allowed this?' She took the pencil she was holding and snapped it in two.

'It's just a minor matter. Some files, relating to an incident years ago.' The man who'd delivered the message could feel the beads of sweat grouping together on his eyebrows.

'How? Who?' Kerrith was spluttering. A bubble of spit glistening on the corner of her red-stained lips.

'Someone who knew the stage-one password. They must have been someone on the inside.'

Kerrith flailed the broken pencil pieces through the air as if she was trying to spear something moving above her. 'And tell me.' Her lips were hardly opening. The words forced out like meat through a mincer. 'Who were the files about?'

'Friedman, ma'am.' The bead of sweat worked loose and rolled slowly down his nose.

Kerrith simply closed her eyes. The pieces of pencil fell to the floor.

'Does it still count as your birthday?' asked Granddad, reaching over and looking at both of Brodie's watches.

Brodie sighed contentedly. They'd been up all evening, chatting and fielding a call from Fabyan and Tandi who rang to wish Brodie a happy birthday and reassure Sheldon and Kitty they were doing all they could to track down Evie from the Elgar Museum. Then they'd spent ages trying to work out an answer to the coded message on the Shepherd's Monument. Between them, they'd come up with nearly twenty acrostics for the Shepherd's Monument letters O U O S V A V V, their favourite being *Octopi Under Orange Seas Vaguely Agree Violet's Vicious*.

Somehow they knew this wasn't the answer.

They'd eaten cake bought from the village shop. Sheldon had sung and Tusia had organised a games tournament, although everyone refused to play chess with her and decided instead on Pictionary, which her team won conclusively anyway. It was the best birthday Brodie could remember. Now everyone had gone to bed, leaving her and Granddad to tidy up.

Brodie considered his question. 'It's past midnight. I guess my birthday's been and gone.'

Her granddad moved to a chair and patted the seat beside him. 'Good. Then it's time to give you this.'

'My present?' said Brodie excitedly.

Her granddad looked a little nervous. 'Maybe,' he said.

She sat down beside him. 'Granddad?'

'There's something I want to give you but I didn't want it to upset you. And I think it will. So I didn't want you to have it on your birthday.'

'Well, don't give me anything that'll upset me – on any day, Granddad,' she said playfully.

He didn't smile. 'Sometimes a thing upsets us, but it's *right*. D'you know what I mean?'

'Like taking medicine?' she said nervously.

'Yes. Like medicine.'

Brodie bit her lip. She hated taking medicine.

Her granddad began to explain. 'Tandi and Fabyan went to the Black Chamber. Seems Tandi managed to override security. She tried to find out what happened to the people who've gone missing. And Friedman.'

'And they've found him?' Brodie could hear the tremor in her own voice. 'They know he's working for the Chamber. That he always was.'

Her granddad put his hand on her arm. 'They did find this.' He reached into his pocket and took out a piece of paper marked with an official stamp. 'They sent it special delivery for you to see.'

'And you think it'll upset me,' she said quietly. 'How can I be more upset than I am? How can this make anything worse?'

He hesitated before he answered. 'It's a statement about what happened the night your mother died. The side of the story Friedman never got to tell you.'

Brodie was sitting on the foot of the stairs, the end of her jumper pulled over her knees. She hadn't changed for bed. There'd been little point. She knew she wouldn't be able to sleep. Not after what she'd read.

She also knew something else.

She couldn't wait any longer.

Since her granddad had left her and made his way upstairs to his room, she'd been thinking. Actually, thinking was too clear a word to explain the way her brain was buzzing and frothing. But she'd made a decision. She couldn't stay.

She took a deep breath and stood up and for a moment she wobbled where she stood. Then she stepped forward, balled her hand into a fist and knocked on the door. 'Kitty. Are you awake? I need your help. Please.'

There was no answer. She called again. Then she turned the handle and stepped inside.

Kitty moved like a bullet released from a gun. She pulled herself up in the bed and sprang on to the mattress, grabbing the bedside lamp and raising it like a weapon. 'I'm armed and dangerous,' she yelled, the bulb flashing on in the lamp and sending a spiral of light swirling across the ceiling. 'I mean it. If you come any closer . . .' The voice tailed away. Kitty lowered the lamp and peered into the gloom. 'Brodie? Is that you?'

Brodie was suddenly aware of movement in the corridor. Hunter was behind her, a shoe raised in his hand. His eyes were wide, his hair a feathered mess around his head. 'Chaos? B? What the midnight feast's going on here? I was sure you were being murdered in your beds.'

'And you thought a shoe would protect us?' retorted Kitty from her standing position on the edge of the mattress. 'Good to know we're in safe hands.'

'Well, a shoe's more use than a bedside lamp that's still plugged in at the wall,' he said mockingly, rubbing his ruffled hair with his free hand. 'What's going on?'

'Ask her,' said Kitty, finally clambering down from the bed. 'She's the one walking around at four o'clock in the morning, scaring people half to death.'

'B?' pressed Hunter. 'What's up?'

Brodie grimaced. The last thing she'd wanted to do

was explain anything to him. Kitty had been her best hope of escape, but Hunter was bound to make things complicated. 'I need a lift,' she said at last, 'on Kitty's bike.'

'A lift? It's the middle of the night. Where on earth d'you want to go?'

'Not sure.' It sounded stupid as she said it.

'D'you eat too much birthday cake, B? Is this a sugar rush like Toots gets when she's heavy on the sherbet?'

Brodie shook her head. Why did he have to get involved?

'Come on, Brodie,' said Kitty, sounding like a supportive aunt. 'What's this about?'

And so she told them.

About the document her granddad had given her. About how it gave Friedman's side of the story.

'So he *was* with your mum when she died. But he was being held captive.' Hunter leant against the window, the shoe still in his hand. 'All this time we thought he'd abandoned your mother when she was dying. But they'd both been hurt. And he'd been made to watch her die.'

'There was a fight,' said Brodie. 'He was beaten trying to get to her. They kept him for weeks, locked in a cell. Then he escaped and wandered for days until someone took him in. And all this time I thought he'd done nothing to help her. But this makes everything different.'

Hunter stopped his pacing. 'But you rang the number, B. You tried to speak to him and he refused your calls. He never came back to tell you any of this. How could you know?'

'But I know now! He wasn't on their side, Hunter. It wasn't his fault. And all this time I've been so angry.' She swallowed and a lump formed thick in her throat.

Hunter looked uncomfortable. He gestured for Kitty to say something.

Kitty folded her arms across her chest and made a small coughing sound. 'I'm sorry,' she said. 'I don't really understand this Friedman thing. It was before my time, I know. But you're saying that now you've read this document you think he never wanted to hurt your mum. But . . .' She hesitated. 'It doesn't mean he didn't change sides afterwards, does it? It might be true that things weren't his fault all that time ago. But where's Friedman now? Why isn't he here to explain?'

'I don't know.' Brodie choked on her words.

'Could it be he's changed sides now?'

Brodie looked down at the floor. The lamp Kitty had held as a weapon was on the ground and the bulb looked blackened as if it had broken in the shaking. As if the light would no longer work.

'You want me to drive you round,' said Kitty, 'trying to find this man so you can talk to him. But it sounds to me that if he wanted to be found, he'd be here.'

Friedman slid his hands down the door. His knuckles were raw.

'I don't know why you keep knocking,' said the old woman seated in the chair behind him. 'You told me yourself they'll never come.'

Freidman didn't face her as he answered. 'I can't give up,' he said.

11

Reflections

They started work early the next morning. Hunter and Kitty said nothing about the night before and when Tusia asked Brodie about the dark shadows under her eyes, she said it was all the excitement of her birthday. She knew Tusia didn't believe her.

Smithies had asked Mrs Hummel if they could use the guest-house sitting room and they'd turned it into a makeshift office, tacking large sheets of paper to the walls, for note taking.

'So,' Smithies said. 'We need to move things forward. Let's think about what we've learnt so far.'

Tusia gave a sigh. 'If we cover everything we'll be here for hours.'

'If we cover everything, we might get an answer.'

Brodie flicked open her notebook. Serious work would make her feel better. But at the moment she wasn't up to sharing. She pushed the notebook along the table towards Hunter. He nodded and took the lead. 'We think the Knights of Neustria left codes and clues for us in their work. And Jaeger, Elgar's friend and one of our most famous Knights, told us to look for clues. So we made a list:

1. Green Fields

2. Quartets

3. Poetry

4. Pictures

'Good,' said Smithies, adding details to the paper behind. 'And that's helped us find things.'

'We think some of the Knights of Neustria were part of a secret society called the Cambridge Apostles,' Hunter continued. 'And that led us to a quartet of graves in Westminster Abbey. And there were poems too, on some of the graves.'

Smithies made a tick against poems and quartets on his list.

'Those graves gave clues about light and darkness and the power of fire. And they talked about secret islands,' said Tusia.

'And a statue led us here to the work of Peter Scheemakers, and his quartet of clues,' rounded up Hunter. He counted them off on his hand as Smithies ticked the list again. 'One was the fireplace, which pointed to the picture of the god of light. Then there's the arch across the green field with the two sculptures of Lord and Lady Anson.' Smithies did more ticking. 'Then the Shepherd's Monument.'

Smithies smiled and raised his pen. 'Brilliant,' he said. 'So. The Shepherd's Monument. A structure with a clear coded message. Makes sense to focus there. Try and find out who the memorial's for and what the letters around the base mean. If we can solve the riddle of the Shepherd's Monument, then who knows? We may finally get the information we need to read MS 408 and that might lead us to Avalon.'

'Simple,' sniffed Sheldon. 'Should have this all sewn up by lunchtime.'

The picture was slightly fuzzy. Tandi peered closer at the screen.

Clues from the Knights of Neustria

Jaegar's List: 1) Green fields ✓
2) Quartet ✓
3) Poetry ✓
4) Pictures ✓

Knights of Neustria ⟨⟨⟨⟩⟩⟩ Linked to Cambridge Apostles

4 memorial stones...

Phoenix   Griffin

Blossom   Tower

↓ ↓   ↓ ↓

Light / Darkness

Fire ~

secret Islands

4 Scheemakers Clues

| Fireplace | Arch-Lord A. | Arch-Lady A. | Shepherd's Monument |

The photo was of a middle-aged man. He was well built, eyes close together. He had a dragon tattoo on his arm.

'I know him!' Tandi fumed. 'Remember! The guard from the gatehouse. Worked here. And then—'

Fabyan moved closer to the screen. 'What's it say about him?'

'That he was working for them,' spat Tandi. 'So that explains how Level Five knew where we were so often.'

'And where is he now?' Fabyan scrolled down the page. 'Does he still work for them?'

'Not according to this.' Tandi pointed at the screen. 'Missing in action. Contract terminated.'

'So could we track him down? Ask some questions?'

'Worth a shot, I guess. Someone round Bletchley might have kept up with him.'

'So who d'we ask?'

Tandi grabbed her coat. 'Gordon,' she said. 'Down at the railway station. He sees everything. Come on. Let's go.'

Hunter pointed to the guidebook Brodie had been given for her birthday. 'Is there stuff about the monument in there?' he said gently. 'We could really do with looking at the picture.'

Brodie took the book and rifled through the pages.

160

She was feeling better. Work *was* making it easier. 'Here,' she said.

'Scheemakers was such an amazing sculptor, look,' said Tusia, flicking to the photo of the tomb. 'There's so much detail.'

'Yeah. Shame he didn't add a scroll to this picture, though,' said Hunter. 'Like the Shakespeare memorials where he sculpted Shakey pointing to the words we were supposed to read.'

'No scroll on this one,' said Tusia. 'Although . . .' She peered in closer. 'Those shepherds.'

'What about them?'

'Well, they're pointing, look, at the tomb and the title *Et in Arcadia Ego*.'

Sheldon peered over her shoulder. 'It's quite precise. Their hands look uncomfortable, as if they're trying to jab at individual letters. See?'

'R and N,' Tusia said. 'D'you think they're important?'

'As important as the whole phrase?' asked Hunter.

'I've been thinking about that,' said Granddad.

'Nice and morbid, isn't it?' said Smithies, casting a look in Sicknote's direction. 'But we hoped the death reference might mean Avalon's real.'

'I like that idea. But the phrase itself. It could mean something else.'

Tusia sat bolt upright. 'It's not one of these things

which can be read in two ways, is it?'

'Well, if it means something also exists in Arcadia, it could mean *the person in the tomb* had also existed there,' said Mr Bray.

'By exist, you mean live?' said Brodie.

'Yes,' said Granddad. 'It could mean the person in the tomb had also lived in this perfect place we hope is Avalon. Perhaps lived there, returned and died. Et in Arcadia Ego. "*I have also existed in Arcadia*".'

'So the monument could be for someone who'd been to Avalon and came back to tell about it?' said Sheldon. 'That would be incredible.'

'So,' said Tusia, pulling the threads together. 'Is there a chance the monument's for a Knight of Neustria who'd found Avalon and returned?'

'Maybe,' said Smithies, resting his glasses on his forehead. 'We could go with that idea and see where it takes us.'

'Brilliant!' said Sheldon. 'But it's no good thinking someone might have been to Avalon and come back if we can't work out who they were.'

'Well, it's got to be someone who was important to the Ansons,' said Brodie.

'What d'we know about their family?' asked Tusia, flicking through the guidebook. 'Oh, look. Here. A picture of Lady Anson. She looks a little sad.'

'What's that in her hand?' Brodie peered in closer.

'Looks like a sketch of something. What's it say?'

Brodie wasn't listening. 'Hold on! Look at what's *on* her hand.'

'No!' yelped Tusia.

Brodie felt the excitement bubble inside her. 'It's a ring. Like *the* ring. Like the one Coleridge wore and the one Sir Francis Bacon hid his code in. It's a Knight of Neustria ring.'

'You sure?' Sheldon grabbed the guidebook.

'What?' snapped Tusia. 'Because she's a girl you think she can't be a Knight!'

'I didn't say that. I was just surprised . . .'

Brodie took the book back. 'So if she's a Knight, we're getting closer! We should look at that picture in her hand, don't you think? Pictures was on Jaeger's list of things we're supposed to be looking for, wasn't it? What *is* the picture she's holding?' She read the explanation beside the text. 'It says it's a sketch she made of the Poussin picture.'

'What, the one Scheemakers copied for the monument?' said Smithies.

'I'm not sure,' said Brodie. She flicked through the book. 'Look, this is the picture copied for the monument.' She pulled away from the text. 'Funny. It looks wrong.'

Tusia pulled a face. 'The monument one has a great big pyramid stuck on top of the tomb and this painted version doesn't. What's that all about? And . . .' Her voice tailed away.

Brodie looked up. Tusia was suddenly walking across the room pointing at the wall. No. Not at the wall. At the mirror hung on the wall.

Brodie felt her stomach lurch. She looked again at the two pictures. 'Oh, I get you! That's it! Look, here's the original picture and here's the one on the monument.' She flicked the book between the two pages.

'It's been reflected!' said Tusia. 'And remember, Lady Anson underlined the phrase *true reflection* in one of her letters. But why do that with the picture on the monument? Why reverse it?'

'Perhaps,' said Brodie, 'it's telling us to use a mirror.' She felt around in her bag to find the present Smithies had given her for her birthday. 'It's the monk in the cell.'

Hunter rolled his eyes and patted Kitty reassuringly on the shoulder. 'She does this. You just have to wait till she talks in a way we can understand. At the moment we've just got to let her mumble.'

'The poem Mrs Hummel read us,' yelped Brodie.

'And when she does this, it's usually about some story or poem she's read,' added Sheldon.

Brodie ploughed on. 'The monk was locked away from the world, wasn't he? And then the poem said:

Through Fancy's flatterine glass he fondly views,
That world, those joys he must for ever lose.

Flatterine glass. Polished glass. A form of window. *Or . . .*' She paused for dramatic effect, holding Smithies' gift in the air. 'A mirror.'

The excitement in the room was like electricity.

'Mrs Hummel said one Latin acrostic using the letters on the tomb was to do with vanity,' cut in Smithies. 'And what d'you spend your time looking in if you're vain?'

'One of these,' beamed Brodie.

'And just in case there's any other doubt, we have to remember all the stuff you told us about Tennyson.' Hunter could barely get the words out quickly enough. 'We've got a quartet of clues! A monk looking through flatterine glass; Lady Anson's underlining about true reflections; a Latin phrase to do with vanity . . . and then we've got that famous mention of the mirror, B banged on about!'

'The Lady of Shalott in the Tennyson poem,' Brodie smiled. 'Mirrors! Loads of mirrors!'

'So,' said Sheldon, grinning widely but his eyes drawn tight in concentration. 'How's that help us? What do we do with the mirrors?'

There was an awkward silence. Tusia moved back to the table and began to doodle on the notebook. She took each letter of the cipher and wrote it again and again, turning the page as she wrote. 'Look at the letter V from the start of the cipher. What'd you notice?'

'Absolutely nothing, Toots.'

'No, look. Here.' Tusia drew the letter again, then took the birthday mirror from Brodie and held it up against the page. 'Can you see? Its reflection?'

'Looks the same to me.'

'That's the point,' Tusia groaned.

'So?'

'Well, you can't do that with every letter in the alphabet. Look at K.' She scribbled on the page. 'And F and G. See? All look wrong if you reflect them. But if you take the letters of the cipher,' she scribbled again, 'they all look the same through the mirror except the letter S.'

'So how's that help?'

'If the picture is reflected, why not the cipher?' Tusia's voice was breathy with excitement. 'The only message anyone can find in the letters written the way they are is something going on about vanity. That's trying to get us to think of a mirror. So maybe the *real* message can only be found when the letters are reflected!'

'I get you, Toots! It's the order that's important if you're looking for an acrostic.' Hunter watched as Tusia scribbled out the cipher the new way round.

'What d'we do with the letter S?' she urged.

'Erm. Go with leaving it out for now,' suggested Smithies. 'There's tiny differences between the picture and the reversal, isn't there? One has a pyramid, one doesn't. So if the letter doesn't reverse then let's leave it out.'

Tusia nodded and finished scribbling the new series of letters. They'd got a new code.

V V A V O U O

12

The Great Darkness

'I can't believe you organised this,' beamed Tusia from the other side of a long trestle table placed down the length of Shugborough Hall library.

'Seems you lot aren't the only ones with special skills,' said Kitty.

'But I still don't understand how you did it,' added Brodie.

Kitty's cheeks flushed a little. 'You tell these National Trust lots you're making a TV programme and you want to make sure all the historical facts are right, and they'll do anything to make sure you do your research properly. I mean, real historians don't want us messing up the details, do they?'

'And we have the private use of this room for how long?' asked Hunter.

'Twenty-four hours,' said Kitty. 'Not bad, eh?'

'It's brilliant,' said Brodie. 'Except, I'm not sure where we start.'

Hunter rolled his eyes. 'Erm. With the books,' he said. 'I'd have thought you'd get that one, B.'

'Obviously we start with the books. But there's so many things to find out about.'

'Break it into pieces,' said Kitty. 'Like service at a pub.'

'Excuse me?'

'When I was working in the Plough, we each had parts of the menu we were responsible for. One of us did starters, one of us the veg. Puddings were down to someone else.'

'And the washing-up was down to me,' huffed Sheldon, who still seemed sore about any references to his life before Veritas.

'Someone had to do it. No clean plates or cutlery and there'd be no food.' Kitty sounded almost like she meant it. 'So we should split this finding out business into chunks too.'

'OK,' agreed Smithies. 'If we're going to try and find out who the Shepherd's Monument's for some of us should look into who lived in the house before it

169

was built and who was important enough for the Ansons to commemorate in a special way.'

'And some of us should focus on the cipher on the base of the tomb. Let's try and work out what the message says,' added Granddad.

'Some should look for other stuff about the Ansons and the buildings they built here and the pictures they owned,' said Tusia. 'And try and track down Lady Anson's ring.'

'And what about the underlining in Lady Anson's letter? It helped us with the mirror idea,' said Brodie. 'We should think about the other stuff she underlined.'

'And we do all that in twenty-four hours,' said Hunter, glancing once again at his watch. 'Piece of cake!'

The Director held the sword. As it sliced through the air, the sound waves hummed.

Kerrith was a little nervous.

The sword was only ornamental. She was at no risk she was sure, but even so, she'd have felt a whole lot better if her boss had put the sword down. Instead, he raised the point in the air and pressed it against his lips. He narrowed his eyes and stared at her. In a draught of sudden coldness, she looked away.

'Things are getting serious,' the Director said, his

words forcing past the tip of the sword still resting against his lips. 'Very serious.'

'You said you wanted us to monitor the team's movement and find out as much as we could about what they made of MS 408,' Kerrith said quietly. She couldn't look at him. If the point of the sword slipped he'd cut himself, she knew it.

There was a moment of silence before the Director answered. His voice was sharp and steely. 'We have perhaps been far too free in our treatment of them.' He spat the word 'them', the idea of a team of people clearly repulsing him. 'I admit, I thought at first allowing them to try and break the code of the manuscript was advisable. Now I'm less sure.'

'Sir?'

He couldn't tell Kerrith he was worried that there'd still been no more deliveries of the scrolls marked with the letter 'T'. He had to find a reason for his nervousness that she'd believe. 'They're drawing people into their web. Their tentacles are reaching out to others and we may do all we can to bring in those they contaminate but the more people exposed to this abomination, the more vulnerable we all become.' He lowered the sword a little and the sunlight glinted on the metal blade.

'So you're suggesting we bring them in now,' mumbled Kerrith, afraid to suggest the wrong thing.

'We stop watching and tracking and we start collecting?'

The Director put the sword on the table. It rocked to and fro. 'No,' he said. 'I'm suggesting something bigger than that.' He needed action that would be noticed.

Kerrith laced her fingers together and waited for him to explain.

'You think, Miss Vernan, that the problem of those who dabble with the prohibited is a *new* problem for the authorities? You think history hasn't been littered with cases of people who've probed too far into the unknown? Reached too deeply into unclear waters? And you think the answer is always as easy as simply "bringing them in"?' There was a sneer in his voice. Kerrith shivered. 'We're the ones with the power, Kerrith. Immense power. World-changing power. Truth-changing power.'

He traced his finger along the blade of the sword.

'Now now, Miss Vernan. You've seen our work in operation, haven't you? You've seen how staff from Level Five of the department have managed, throughout time, to suppress that which needs suppressing, to hide what must remain hidden. And we've employed all the agents of history to do our work.'

Kerrith's fingers tightened together.

'1912,' said the Director. 'The year the manuscript

was found. The year MS 408 came to light. Don't you think we had a strategy to cope with such a find? A technique to deal with a rediscovery of a document we'd spent decades trying to insist didn't exist.' He was enjoying this part of the explanation. 'History's got a way of offering diversions, Miss Vernan, if you employ it carefully.'

'Diversions, sir?'

The Director nodded. 'In 1912, when the manuscript was rediscovered, there were those who suggested they had answers. We needed a diversion. A world event which would take the focus from the find. A "disaster" to shock the world.'

'A world event, sir?'

'We control history, Kerrith. If we have to lose a few lives to maintain order and peace, then we do what we must do.' He angled his head to look at her more clearly. 'Forty years later, in 1952, we had new reason to hide the truth. Darkness,' he said coldly. 'That's a great way to hide.'

She was thoroughly confused now, but wise enough to know admitting this fact wouldn't be the safest move. 'You're suggesting, sir,' she faltered onwards, 'instead of simply bringing in the Veritas team, we do something to distract from any discovery they might make. Something to cause a cover for removing them.'

The Director raised the sword once more from the table. 'You catch on quickly, Miss Vernan.'

'And in 1912, sir? And in 1952 you drew attention away from the discovery of MS 408 and the work being done on it by code-crackers, how exactly?'

The Director paused, the sword held momentarily in the air. Then he plunged it deep into the stone base on his desk. 'You need to check your history books, Miss Vernan. All you need to know is there.'

'I'm telling you there's no answers in these books,' wailed Hunter, banging his forehead against the mound of volumes encircling him at the end of the trestle table.

'You shouldn't give up so easily,' encouraged Tusia.

Hunter banged his head again with even more vigour. 'Give up easily,' he mimicked. 'We've been at this for 374 minutes. How the stuffed marrow can that be giving up too easily?'

At the end of the table, Sicknote winced a little as Hunter continued to bang his head, but no one bothered to answer him. He had, after all, been making the same comments for at least half an hour and little anyone said seemed to encourage him.

Brodie tried to ignore Hunter's moaning and circled the other two underlined phrases she'd taken from Lady

Anson's letter again and again so the pen-nib nearly scored through the page.

How on earth was this supposed to help her? She'd searched through books giving details on the work of silkworms making thread and the history of surely every fountain that'd ever been written about. One book on architecture left. Maybe that could tell her about the fountain of true love. She scrolled down the index, skimmed through a chapter on ancient clock towers which was full of interesting pictures, then turned to page 176. A whole section on Rome.

'I'm telling you, I'm dying here,' whined Hunter. 'Second by second, little pieces of me are dying.'

'And we'll be sure to write an essay on your grave about what a hero you were,' said Tusia. 'And how you never made a fuss and kept working until the bitter end.'

'Oh, OK, Toots. Sorry if my dying's disturbing you. I'll try and die a little more quietly if you'd just allow me to get it over with.' He banged his head again on the table and the pile of books shuddered.

'Probably wouldn't be room to write all that on his grave,' mumbled Sicknote. 'If you think about it, they tend to restrict what's written to the most important details. That's why we're struggling with this tomb!'

Mr Bray looked up from the book he was reading. 'Might be on to something there, Oscar. What d'you write on a grave?'

'Name of the person. But we haven't got that,' offered Tusia.

'Date of birth and death,' said Hunter. 'No joy there either.'

'And who they were,' said Kitty awkwardly. 'Mother, sister, wife, that sort of thing.'

'Exactly . . . so what about "My Daughter"?'

Smithies winced then shook his head. 'These books don't list the Ansons as having one.'

'But I've been thinking about this reversed cipher. And how maybe the other letters on the base of the tomb should be read in reverse too,' said Mr Bray.

'You mean the DM stuff?' offered Tusia.

'Yes. Why just reflect the cipher? If we reverse DM then we have MD. And that could stand for "My Daughter".' His voice cracked a little and he looked down at the pages spread across the table. 'It was just an idea.'

Tusia patted his hand gently. 'But Smithies just explained the Ansons didn't have one.'

'Could be someone else's daughter,' offered Brodie,

smiling encouragingly at her granddad. 'Someone so special the Ansons *treated* her like a daughter.'

'OK. But where'd she come from? This special girl?' asked Tusia.

Silence again. Brodie looked back down at her notes and the open book in front of her. 'Oh, wait a minute. Look at this. It's a long shot. But keep with me.' She looked back at her notes from earlier. 'Lord Anson founded the Dilettanti Society in 1732. Well, it says here, at the exact same time, building began on a famous fountain. *A fountain of true love.* That's one of the other phrases underlined in Lady Anson's letter.'

'And that fountain's here at Shugborough?' asked Sheldon.

'No.' Brodie tried not to sound despondent. 'It's in Italy. Rome. It's called the Trevi Fountain. This book says, according to legend, if you throw three coins into the fountain you'll find true love and return to Rome.'

'Nice,' said Hunter.

'Here's a picture,' said Brodie, pushing forward the book she'd flipped open on the page. 'So, if this was the fountain of true love, then maybe someone who was important to the Ansons, who they treated like a daughter, came once from Italy to stay with them and then returned to Rome.'

'OK,' said Sicknote cautiously. 'Suppose we go with

that idea, to connect the two underlined phrases, and the reversing of the letters. Anyone found any reference to Italy in what they've read?'

Smithies pressed his hands on the table. 'Here, look. I'm working through a copy of a family logbook. It's got a list of guests to Shugborough. I've been trying to work out if any were important.'

'Any Italians?'

Smithies skim-read the pages, muttering names under his breath. 'One, here, see!'

'Well, go on then,' said Hunter, straining forward, the pink mark on his head now a darker red.

'A woman came from Italy. Taken in by the family and stayed with them for a while.'

'Was she like a daughter to them?' asked Sheldon hopefully.

Smithies flicked through the pages. 'Erm . . . Says she was called Lucia Narora. Stayed here at Shugborough.' He ran his finger along the page. 'But she didn't come alone. Says she brought a child with her.'

'She *had* a daughter then?' asked Tusia excitedly.

'Yes! A girl called Renata. She was only a few years old.'

Smithies muttered aloud as he read, flicking page after page. 'There's lots here about Lucia Narora and her daughter Renata staying for several years. Says they were even given their own servant here. Someone called Thomas Jefferson Beale. But wait a minute.' He flicked the pages again. 'Lucia went back to Rome. It says so.'

'Well, I told you. The legend about the fountain says you will go back,' said Brodie. 'But what about the daughter?'

'Erm. Says the girl got ill. No one knew what was wrong with her. They tried everything. Herbal remedies; wrapping her in gold and silk; all sorts of crazy stuff.' He looked up from the page. 'Nothing worked. And they lost her.'

'She died? At Shugborough?' asked Sicknote.

Smithies nodded.

'So does it say where she's buried?' asked Kitty.

Smithies had kept reading. 'It just says, after the death of her daughter, Lucia and the servant Thomas Jefferson Beale returned to Italy. Doesn't mention if Lucia took her daughter back to be buried. But it doesn't make sense for her to do that. All that travelling. It's more logical to bury her here.'

'Anything else?' pressed Brodie. 'About when she died?'

'Nope. Just those failed remedies.'

'Let me see,' said Sicknote. He took the book and then looked across the table at Brodie. 'Oh, well done, Brodie.'

Brodie pulled a face. 'I haven't . . .'

Sicknote grabbed for her notes and smiled at the frantic circling on the page. 'Lady Anson's underlining! It says they wrapped the child up. In *gold and silk.* That's the third phrase underlined in the letter.'

'Brilliant!' said Hunter. 'This Renata Narora *could* be the one the monument's for.'

'What d'you think?' said Brodie keenly. 'It's a possibility, isn't it?'

Granddad pushed himself to standing. His smile was broad and wide. 'Oh, I'd say it was more than a possibility.'

'Why? We've just linked the stories of the fountain and the death of a child. It doesn't mean it's true.'

'Maybe not,' said Granddad, 'if Smithies hadn't included the details about the name.'

Brodie felt her forehead furrow into lines.

'Lucia's child. She was called Renata?'

Smithies nodded.

'Well, Renata has a special meaning. It translates as "reborn".'

'And reborn could mean like a phoenix or a firebird,' blurted Tusia.

Granddad smiled in agreement. 'But even if it didn't mean that, then the letters of her name are enough.' He reached across the table and picked up a book, flicking through it until he found a picture of the Shepherd's monument. 'Remember?' he said, pointing at the shepherd's fingers. 'The letters they're pointing to?'

Brodie took the book from him.

It was clear to see. Two outstretched hands. Two letters.

R and N.

Brodie let her mouth slide over the letters of the name of the Italian child, christened after the phoenix. 'Renata Narora. R and N.'

'It's her,' she said. 'The person commemorated by the Shepherd's Monument. I think we've found her.'

Gordon put down three cream puffs on the table beside the pot of tea that was already steaming. 'Haven't seen Smithies for ages,' he said. 'Or Friedman. They're OK, I take it.'

Fabyan shuffled on his chair. 'Things are good, Gordon. Always good. And by the way, we owe you big time for your help with the zebras. Nice work. I hope you'd be ready to help us out again if we ever need cover.'

Gordon smiled and took a bite of his cream puff. A cloud of icing sugar wafted in front of his face. 'Got a soft spot for zebras,' he said. 'The stripes, I guess. Look a bit like railway tracks.'

'See, the thing is, Gordon,' said Tandi, toying with the edge of her own pastry. 'We're trying to make contact with one of the guards who used to work at Bletchley. Things got a little awkward. There was a misunderstanding and . . . well, you know how it is.'

Gordon nodded through another cloud of icing sugar.

Fabyan took out the print out of the guard's photo and put it on the table. 'I'm sure you remember him.' He pointed at the dragon tattoo. 'Quite distinctive-looking guy.'

Gordon downed the last of his pastry. 'Sure. I remember him. Fell on hard times, so I hear.'

'Hard times?'

'Yeah. Last time I saw him he was hanging around Campbell Park in Milton Keynes. I'm not sure he told his wife, see, about losing his job with you. You could look for him there.'

'You think he hangs around in a park all day?' asked Tandi.

'I think he likes to keep out of his wife's way,' explained Gordon with a knowing wink. 'It's a big park.'

Tandi pushed her plate into the middle of the table. 'You've been brilliant,' she said.

* * *

Smithies ran his hand across his chin. 'So we think we know who the monument was for. But we still need to solve the other puzzles of the tomb.'

'Fair point,' said Granddad. 'I've told you, I'm on to those letters. I'm doing the best I can. I really am.'

'We'll help with the letters, Granddad,' encouraged Brodie. She took a new piece of paper and wrote out the title 'Et in Arcadia Ego'. Then she added the flipped-round cipher from below.

Tusia leant forward and circled the word 'Arcadia' in the title.

'What'd you do that for?' asked Brodie.

'Arcadia. We think it means Avalon, don't we? That Renata had been to Avalon.'

'Arcadia, Avalon. Some sort of perfect place.'

Tusia circled the word again, then she tightened the circle so it only linked round the 'A'. 'Arcadia, Avalon. They both begin with A.'

'So? Loads of words begin with A, Toots. Apples, Anchovies, Almonds.'

'Food words – what a shocker! Both of mine are words for a perfect place. They both relate to the Knights of Neustria. That's all. I was just saying.'

'Suppose we use that?' said Sheldon. 'I mean, use the word Arcadia or Avalon. In the cipher?'

'How?' asked Hunter.

'The cipher could say something about how Renata went to Avalon and returned.'

'OK,' said Smithies, rubbing his hands. 'So perhaps now we ask about when she went to Avalon.' He looked back down at the family logbook. 'These entries are for some time after 1750. That's when Lucia and Renata arrived at Shugborough. So any visit to Avalon must have been before then. Does that help anyone? Any important dates around that time?'

'1743,' suggested Hunter.

Everyone looked along the table at him.

'Gonna have to give us more than that,' joked Sheldon.

'1743. That's when Lord Anson captured the Spanish treasure ship the *Covadonga*.'

'So what you saying?' said Brodie.

'I'm saying,' said Hunter, 'maybe there's a chance Lucia and Renata were on the *Covadonga*. Perhaps Lord Anson met them then and suggested they come to Shugborough with him.'

'It's a good idea,' said Brodie. 'Links all we know. But d'you think it means the *Covadonga* had been to Avalon, then?'

'Could do,' said Tusia. 'And you know what else it could mean, if that's true?'

'What?'

Et in (A)rcadia Ego

R N = Renata Narora?

OUOSVAVV _____ cipher

(A)rcadia = (A)valon

1743

→ Capture of
The Covadonga

✳ Were Lucia and Renata on the
Covadonga?

✳ Did the Covadonga go to Avalon?

I bet it did!

'That maybe the treasure captured was Avalon treasure.'

'You think the treasure on the *Covadonga* was *from* Avalon?' Brodie pressed.

'Could be,' said Hunter. His voice was lifting with excitement. 'Mrs Hummel said Lord Anson was obsessed with tracking that ship. Wouldn't give up even though all the other ships in his fleet were lost. It must have been really special treasure to keep him hunting.'

'So what do we do, then?' asked Tusia.

'We keep working,' Hunter said.

'But I thought you said you were tired and we'd been at it too long.'

'That was before I realised how close we are. We're nearly there. I can sense it. We've found the monument of someone who might actually have been to Avalon. We might have found connections to treasure from Avalon. We have to keep going. We've got to work out what those letters on the tomb say.'

It was Granddad's turn to beat his forehead against the table. 'I'm on it,' he yelped. 'I keep telling you. I'm trying as hard as I can.'

13

The Human Code

Brodie woke to the sound of yelling.

She lifted her head from the table and a pencil fell from an indentation in her cheek, although a crumpled page of notes remained firmly attached, glued into position with a fair amount of drool.

'What?'

She tried to focus and batted away the crinkled paper, wiping her mouth with the back of her hand.

They were still in the library. The light was dim, a single lamp alight in an alcove. At the end of the table, Sheldon was snoring loudly.

Brodie scanned the room to find the source of the noise which had woken her. It was Granddad and Sicknote. They were standing at the other end of the table, faces reflected in the bookcase mirrors, eyes wide, hands open. And they were shouting. 'We've got it. We've got it. We've really got it.'

Brodie rubbed her face and blinked her eyes. 'What time is it? How long have we . . .'

Granddad knocked her questions away. 'We've worked out the code. We think we know what the letters stand for.'

It took only moments for everyone to wake. Brodie gulped from a bottle of water, now warm. 'Go on, Granddad,' she urged.

'It was what Tusia said earlier about the letter A that did it,' he said slowly. 'Brodie worked it out last time, about Bensalem not being a person but being a place. And it was a place Sir Francis Bacon had written about. In a book.'

Brodie felt her forehead smooth. 'I see where you're going with this,' she said. 'It's the title of the book, isn't it?' she said.

Mr Bray nodded. 'The story was about Bensalem, but it was in a book with a different title. Sir Francis called his book *New Atlantis*.'

'The letter A again,' said Sheldon. 'Now I'm with you.'

'Maybe the choice of the letter A is important,' said Mr Bray. 'It could mean *Atlantis* or *Arcadia* or *Avalon*.

The words can be interchanged but the letter A remains.'

'So what does that mean?' asked Hunter.

Granddad took a piece of paper from the table and scribbled a series of letters across the page. 'We think the letters on the monument have to be read in reverse because of all the mirror clues we've read. Agreed?'

There was a general mumble around the table.

'So we're left with VVAVOUO. We're looking for a coded message with those letters and our problem was where to start. I mean, the message could have been in English, or it could have been in another language and if that was the case then how on earth would we make sense of it?'

'But you *have* made sense of it?' said Brodie.

Sicknote rattled the chain which connected his mug to the radiator. 'We went for Latin. That had to be the most logical language for the inscription. And it was the least I could do to try it out.'

'If the letter A stood for Avalon or Atlantis or Arcadia we suddenly had more to work with,' said Granddad. 'And if we put the word 'Avalon' into the code as a place name, then we're getting somewhere . . . Look.'

He took the pen and scribbled a new line of letters on the paper, this time completing the word 'Avalon' after the letter A.

V V Avalon V O U O.

'Now we're left with six letters to complete the acrostic. I needed to find Latin words beginning with the six remaining letters which would make sense when spoken together in a phrase.'

'So how d'you do that?' asked Brodie, who was trying hard to remain patient.

'Well, there's loads of well-known Latin phrases. We use them all the time.'

'*You* might,' said Hunter. 'Can't say I slip into Latin very often.'

'Oh, but you'll have heard the phrases,' cut in Granddad. 'Like *carpe diem*, which means "seize the day" and make the most of your opportunities. Or *a cappella* which means—'

'When a song is sung without music accompaniment,' interrupted Sheldon. 'I get you.'

'It's not just the world of medicine which relies on Latin phrases, you know,' offered Sicknote. '*Ad infinitum* is another example.'

'Which means "to infinity",' said Hunter. 'OK, I see your point. We use more Latin than we realise. And so?'

'And so, I went through all of the Latin phrases I knew and found one that fitted.'

'And you're sure it's not a coincidence? You haven't made a phrase fit just because you can?'

Sicknote looked a little aggrieved. 'Translations from Latin are tricky. There's always alternatives for words but I don't think I've done that. For two reasons.' He counted them off on his fingers as he spoke. 'Firstly, what are the chances of stumbling on a Latin phrase using those letters when the letter choice is so limited?'

Smithies angled his head to the side. 'I suppose Vs and Os don't give you that much scope.'

'Exactly. But then, more than that, when you hear the phrase it just has to be the one that fits.' He pressed the second finger of his hand.

'So what's the phrase?'

'OK, the V and V first. I think those two Vs stand for the phrase *Veritas vincit.*'

'Veritas?' said Brodie. 'As in Truth? Like in the name of Operation Veritas?'

Granddad nodded his head.

'And the *vincit* then?' asked Tusia.

Sicknote drew himself up tall. '*Veritas vincit* means "Truth conquers".'

'And the other letters?' pressed Hunter. 'After the A for Avalon.'

'The letters V O U O could stand for the phrase *Verum opprimo umbra occasus.*

No one spoke. All waited for him to explain.

'So *Avalon's verum opprimo umbra occasus* means "Avalon's truth suppresses the shadow of sunset".'

'Suppresses?' said Brodie quietly. Her mind was churning. She remembered the Guildhall Library and the restricted section of books. And the mark of those who hid books.

Granddad nodded slowly. 'We know there's a team of people who've tried to hide works of writing. We know they call themselves the Suppressors. But if we're right, the writing on the tomb could mean the truth of Avalon will suppress the false truth those people try to promote.'

'And the sunset bit?' asked Tusia.

'It fits with Jaeger's Sunshine,' said Sicknote. 'And the writing on the Shakespeare monument in Leicester Square. Sunset's a time when light fades. When shadows form. The whole search we've been following has been based on finding the light.'

'It's like the story of Plato's Cave all over again,' smiled Smithies. 'There's a truth and it's better than the shadows we're being made to watch.'

'So that's what the phrase on the tomb could mean, then,' said Brodie. 'There's a truth out there. A truth from Avalon. And that truth will suppress the ignorance the Suppressors are trying to promote.'

Mr Bray folded his arms. 'Exactly.'

Veritas vincit. Avalon verum opprimo umbra occasus.
Truth conquers. The truth of Avalon suppresses the
shadow of sunset.

It had taken three days of walking round Campbell
Park to find him. Tandi's feet were killing her, not just
from the walking but from the running. Seemed their
missing gate guard wasn't keen to chat. But Fabyan was
surprisingly quick on his feet, despite his red leather
boots, and eventually the man with the dragon tattoo
agreed to talk to them.

'The old guy. He warned me off. Made me think
I was best off getting out.'

'Mr Bray made you leave your job at Station X?' said
Tandi, stifling her surprise.

'He went on about his granddaughter and I got
thinking about my family. And I just didn't feel it was
right any more, working as a double-agent. I don't
understand what you lot are up to. And I don't know
the details of what Level Five are doing. But it felt
wrong. You get me?'

Tandi nodded. 'Oh, we get you.'

'So you're going to punish me for passing them
information?' he asked.

'No. That's not why we're here.'

The guard looked more shocked than relieved.

'We're just trying to find out where they may have taken people. Missing people, I mean. There are some friends we're trying to track.'

'I don't know anything about that. I'm just trying to keep myself off their radar. If they found me, then . . .' He shuddered.

'So you've got no idea where the missing people are taken?'

He shook his head. 'All I know is there were whispers. People would go on about how you'd never want to get sent down.' He emphasised the last word as if it was important.

'Sent down. That means "sent to prison", doesn't it?'

'It meant more than that. I don't know what. But it did.'

Fabyan smiled. 'You've been very helpful,' he said. Tandi wasn't altogether sure this was true. As far as she was concerned, they'd learnt nothing new.

'You should be careful,' she said, getting up from the bench they'd been sitting on. 'I'm pretty sure Level Five will be looking for you. I'm not so sure they'd take being double-crossed quite as calmly as we did. I don't think you get to walk out of the Chamber and really get away.'

The man's eyes darkened. 'I know. But at least now I'm free.'

'It's more proof of the conspiracy, isn't it?' said Hunter, squinting his eyes against the sun. 'A plan to hide the truth that's been going on for hundreds of years?'

They were outside in the grounds of Shugborough Hall, trying to shake off the remnants of a night of dozing and working. And of finding answers. They'd returned to the guest-house to wash and freshen up and then, under Mrs Hummel's guidance, had packed up a picnic breakfast to take to the grounds. They were, she suggested, looking like they all needed a dose of fresh air.

Smithies led the way back to the Shepherd's Monument and they sat now, facing it, munching enthusiastically on sausage sandwiches and pastries Mrs Hummel had prepared for them, Hunter kindly making quick work of Tusia's sausage sandwich once he'd found the vegetarian pasty Mrs Hummel had also packed in case.

'Well, the Knights of Neustria wouldn't have needed to be a secret organisation if it was OK for them to talk freely about what they knew,' confirmed Sicknote.

'It's kind of scary though, isn't it?' said Tusia. 'Seeing the warning written in black and white on something so old.' She glanced across at the monument where the string of letters stared back, unmoving.

'This Avalon must be an incredible place if people are so keen to make us believe it doesn't exist,' said Hunter. 'You reckon we'll ever work out enough to actually find it?'

Brodie put down her sandwich and stretched her arms. They ached. She was exhausted. Her mind felt foggy. Full of shadows. If so much secrecy existed about Avalon, if so many clues about where it was had to be cloaked in mystery, were they really up to the challenge of continuing? She leant back and looked at the monument. She wondered about the child Renata who it was built for. Maybe a child who'd actually seen Avalon.

'Who's that?' said Tusia, dusting pastry crumbs off her shirt.

'Pardon?'

'I said, who's that?' she said again, pointing into the air.

Brodie followed the line of her gaze. Carved at the top of the monument, above the pillars, in the middle of the stone frieze, was the shape of a man's head with horns. Brodie sifted the stories in her head. 'I think it's the god Pan, isn't it?' she grinned.

Smithies nodded.

'And that makes you smile, why?' asked Hunter, gesturing towards Tusia's pasty, silently asking if she'd finished with it.

'Because he's the god of hunting,' Brodie said deliberately. 'And that fits, doesn't it? That the truth needs hunting for.'

'So you're not tempted to give up, then?' said Smithies.

Brodie shook her head.

'Because I think if we're going to keep hunting for the truth then we haven't finished here at Shugborough.'

'Haven't we?' said Tusia, passing the pasty to Hunter with an intense look of disdain on her face.

'Any ideas what we look at next?' asked Smithies.

'Well, I want to look at that tower we saw. There's something about it which bothered me. Can we take another look?'

Hunter hurried to gulp down the pasty. 'Lead the way, B,' he said. 'You just head on and the hunt continues.'

'Erm, if I might just be allowed a moment of your time?' Sicknote was hurrying behind them trying to catch up. He was dabbing his forehead with a handkerchief as he walked.

Brodie slowed her pace.

'I understand your determination to continue, Brodie,' he said, stowing the handkerchief in his back pocket. 'The situation with your mother, of course, is going to spur you on.' He looked down a little to the ground, his eyes flicking from side to side. 'But if I could drop in a note of caution.'

Brodie stopped walking altogether.

'If you'd indulge me a moment and allow me to give a little history lesson.'

'Go on,' said Brodie.

Sicknote took a small bottle from his pocket, gobbled two tablets and then cleared his throat before speaking. 'Codes are dangerous things,' he said. 'They have the potential to change lives. In 1953 two scientists named Watson and Crick cracked a code. The human code.' He watched her face for a moment. 'They discovered DNA, the code by which our genetic imprint is passed on. The secret to our physical existence.'

'We went to that pub, in Cambridge, didn't we?' said Tusia. 'The place where they announced their discovery.'

'Indeed,' said Sicknote, tightening the necktie belting his pyjama trousers. 'A place worth remembering. But with that great discovery announced there came a great responsibility.'

'Why?' asked Kitty.

'Well, if you discover the coded secrets of physical life then what do you do with that knowledge? How much do you use the code and manipulate what's found?'

'I don't understand,' said Brodie.

'Understanding DNA meant scientists could make decisions about life and alter genes.'

'But for good reasons,' said Tusia defensively. 'To help people.'

'Of course. Of course. For the greater good. But it's not that simple. Look, it might be a good thing to play around with DNA if you're trying to find cures for terrible diseases, but when does it stop? When are scientists responsible for doing too much?'

'Playing God?' said Sheldon.

Sicknote nodded. 'With great discoveries comes the responsibility to decide what to do with that knowledge. How far to explore the truth.'

'So why are you saying this now?' pressed Brodie.

Sicknote wrung his hands together. 'Until we came to Shugborough, I suppose I thought it was just a theory that Avalon existed. But now we're following ideas that suggests Renata actually went there. That there really were people who journeyed to this place and returned.' He looked sad suddenly. 'I'm an old man. My health's not what it was. You tell me you'll keep hunting the truth and I have to ask where you think you'll stop. I know we talked before about how people have always been searching for Avalon. But if we're right about what we've worked out, then the monument changes things.'

Brodie waited before she spoke. 'I suppose it does.'

Sicknote ran the handkerchief across his face again. 'I just want to know how far we're going to take this hunt.'

The air was crisp with expectation. 'You mean, will we really try and find out where Avalon is?' Brodie said.

Sicknote waited before he answered. 'I'm scared perhaps you won't.'

Brodie tried not to show her surprise.

'Scared you won't try to get there,' he said at last. 'I'm old and tired. And I need to know you'll keep going with this adventure right to the end. All the way to Avalon. I need to know you won't back out.'

'Of course we won't. We'll keep going.'

Sicknote waited for a moment. 'Whatever the cost?'

Brodie peered at the face of the man in front of her, his eyes wide as he scanned her face for confirmation. 'Yes.'

'Good, then I want to show you something else from the library last night.'

Tower of the Winds

'My phone,' yelped Brodie.

'You left it behind,' said Sicknote.

Brodie felt a little awkward. Smithies had told her to be sure she looked after it. She was certain she and Kitty had tidied everything away from the tables as they left.

'You need to make sure you always know where this is,' said Sicknote in his best attempt to be stern. 'Level Five, you know. We can't afford to take chances.'

'I'm sorry. I'm sure I—'

'It doesn't matter. What matters is the message Tandi sent last night.'

Brodie grabbed for the phone. It didn't bother her that Sicknote had read the message. They'd agreed the phone was for all of them. A way of keeping in touch. She was only keen to see what had been said.

Sicknote swung the phone out of reach. 'You sure you want to see?'

Brodie reached again for it.

Tandi had sent a text. It was short as if she'd typed it in a hurry.

Hope document we sent helped you, Brodie ☺ Things here not looking that good ☹
Found lots of details about missing people. Mr Willer gone. Can't find Evie or Miss Longman. Having trouble getting hold of Les again. Let Smithies know.
Hope things are going better for you. GTGN.
Keep safe!

'Les? Who's he?' asked Tusia, once she'd read the message over Brodie's shoulder.

'A cleaner at Level Five. A contact. He's probably the one who's been helping Tandi get inside to look at what she needs to.'

'And you think this means Level Five have worked out what she and Fabyan are up to?' asked Hunter.

The look on Sicknote's face was the only answer they needed.

* * *

Brodie reached for the locket round her neck. It was strangely comforting. 'I was bothered by this place,' she said, looking up at Anson's tower. 'Something felt wrong about it when we were here.' She tried not to think about things not being right with Tandi and Fabyan. She knew they just had to plough on.

'Could certainly do with a lick of paint,' said Smithies. Brodie knew he was also trying not to worry.

Brodie twisted the locket and looked behind her. Maybe that was it. It seemed odd the tower looked in need of a little care. But that couldn't be all, surely? When did she ever care about paintwork?

She twisted her hand once more and the sunlight flashed for a second on the silver backing of the locket. Sunlight. The key to all the clues. Sunlight and mirrors.

She ran quickly to where Smithies had rested the picnic hamper and began to search.

'I don't think the answer's another pastry, Brodie,' called Tusia. 'You need to find yourself something which releases carbohydrates a little more slowly. Steady fuel. Like a banana.'

Brodie rummaged deeper.

'Afraid I ate the last one on the journey up in the Matroyska,' confessed Hunter.

'Ahha,' said Brodie, pulling out the birthday mirror.

'Your hair looks OK,' said Hunter. 'I mean, I prefer

it when it's up in that sort of twisted plait but what you've done today is fine.'

Brodie made a face and then jumped to her feet. She held the mirror and angled the silver-edged looking-glass up towards the sun so light flashed from the surface. 'I used to do this all the time in maths lessons,' she said.

'You used to play with mirrors in maths lessons!' groaned Hunter.

'When we had to do that whole symmetry thing and draw the other side of the shape. I used to try and reflect the sun around using the mirror.'

'Oh, I know,' said Kitty. 'I've done it with a watch. Tried to make the reflection bounce off the teacher's face.'

'You kids really ought to have paid more attention in school,' offered Granddad.

'Well, if we had, we wouldn't be here now, looking at this, would we?' said Brodie, angling the mirror upwards.

Hunter stepped closer. 'What? The reflection of the sky?'

Brodie angled the mirror a little to the left. 'No. Look. The reflection of the top of the tower.'

Hunter looked down. 'Oh, I see. I get it.'

'You do?'

'No. Not really. I'm just saying that to make you feel better, B. I've no idea what I'm supposed to be looking at.'

'The mirror just lets you focus. See things closer up. So what can you see reflected in the mirror?'

'The top of the tower,' said Hunter.

'And what about the top of the tower?'

Hunter peered in. 'Well, I guess it could do with a paint job too. It's looking a little flaky.'

'Exactly,' said Brodie with such enthusiasm it made the mirror shake. 'I bet there's something painted underneath the flaky topcoat.' She passed the mirror round so the others could see as she began to explain.

Hunter held the mirror now.

'Maybe the truth's just hidden in plain sight,' Brodie said.

'Best sort of secret,' said Smithies.

'I don't get it,' said Sheldon, fiddling with his silent harmonica. 'Why are you so sure the tower contains a secret?'

'I don't know,' said Brodie. 'It was just an idea.' She was thinking back to the book on architecture she'd been searching through, looking for information on fountains. There'd been something about towers. She was trying to remember. She ran her hands across her face and as she did, the straps of her two wristwatches banged together. 'Clock tower,' she said suddenly. 'An ancient clock tower.'

'But there's no clock, B,' Hunter said gently.

'I know. I know. And that's OK. Because there wouldn't be a clock face because this tower has eight sides.'

Hunter raised one eyebrow. 'Why's that important?'

Brodie tried to see the page she'd read again in her mind. 'I read something about how most normal clock towers have four sides. But if a tower had eight sides then it was based on the very first clock tower. It had a special name.'

'She's right,' said Sicknote. 'The very first clock tower was called the Tower of the Winds.'

'Look at this.' Tandi had printed a page from the computer. She was flapping it in her hand.

'More on Friedman?' said Fabyan, taking the page from her. 'You know where he is?'

'No. But look.' She pointed to a sentence written below his name on the printout: *Sent Down*.

'But Friedman didn't go to prison. That's the point, isn't it? If "sent down" means "sent to prison". He was freed and the whole problem is, he didn't come back to the team.'

'I know. But the guard in the park. With the dragon

206

tattoo. He said you didn't want to get *Sent Down*. Maybe "Down" means something else. Maybe there really is a reason Friedman didn't come back to us.'

'Here it is. I knew it.' They were back in the library and Brodie was standing with her hands pressed down hard on the open pages of a large reference book. 'I saw it while I was looking for stuff on fountains earlier. I knew I hadn't imagined it.'

The rest of the team huddled round her, peering at the pages.

'We know the Ansons and their Society of Dilettanti liked all the Greek stuff,' went on Brodie.

'The architecture, you mean?' chipped in Tusia.

'Yes. The buildings. They built copies of things all over the place.'

'Like that triumphal arch for starters?' said Tusia.

'Exactly. Based on a real arch. Some Greek design. So maybe the tower's based on another design. Something old and Greek.'

Sicknote took the book and began to skim-read the writing. 'Here we go. Says here the original Tower of the Winds was called the *Andronikos Crryhestes*. Was built in Athens and was the world's very first clock tower.' He held the book up so everyone could see the picture. 'It was an octagonal building and on every side

207

was a sundial to show the time.'

'Sun again,' hissed Tusia, in case the reference was lost on anybody.

'Inside the tower there was also a water clock.'

'Don't say it, Toots,' smiled Hunter, lifting his hand to silence her. 'There's the water reference.'

'And on the top of the tower there was a wind vane. Now, in the original version there was a frieze running along the top of the tower showing the four great winds. They called them the Anemoi.' He waited for them to catch up. 'Maybe that's our clue.'

'Clue to what?' said Hunter

Sicknote ploughed on. 'Like Brodie said, the tower outside in the grounds looks just like any old tower, but if there's a frieze or painting around the top of the building then that makes the tower a Tower of the Winds.'

'And why would that make all the difference?' Tusia asked tentatively.

Brodie wasn't really sure either. It seemed like such a good idea but she wasn't sure how it could help them.

Sicknote put the book back down on the table. 'Where else have we seen a tower?'

'Erm, Lady of Shalott poem?' offered Sheldon.

'Excellent. Where else? Another picture of a tower?'

'Westminster Abbey,' cut in Tusia. 'On the

Is this a tower of the winds?

Andronicus Cyrrhestes

↓

Athens

↓

World's first clock tower

Octagonal building → Sundial → Water clock → Wind vane

⬇

Four Great Winds - the Anemon

East wind

North wind

West wind

South wind

gravestone on the floor.'

'Brilliant. So what was special about that image?'

'Well, it was on fire. Or at least there was smoke or light or something pouring out of it,' said Kitty.

'Fire maybe,' said Sicknote. 'Or light. Or even wind.'

'I get it!' jumped in Sheldon. 'We thought the tower was on fire. But maybe the picture was really showing swirls of wind.'

'Precisely! And you've already said how important towers have been in this search. Without the Lady of Shalott in her tower, we'd never have worked out the clue on the Shepherd's Monument!'

'So we came here to Shugborough to try and make connections to what we found in Westminster Abbey,' said Tusia, 'and there may really be a link between the tower here and the gravestone!'

Smithies nodded and passed her the open book. 'You should look at this sketch of the four winds, before we set off and see if we can find them hiding under the paint of the tower. I'm guessing they're there. And that's a message for us.'

The Director slammed his desk drawer shut. This was getting ridiculous. How long was he supposed to wait until he heard? There'd been no messages for weeks.

He reached across the desk for the paperweight and pulled the sword from the stone. This action made him feel a little better. But not much.

He drew the desk drawer open again with the blade. The scrolls were there, taunting him.

As he looked at them, he pressed the tip of the sword against the heel of his thumb. He felt no pain as a tear of blood splashed down on the topmost scroll.

15

The Road to Hyperborea

'I cannot believe we're doing this in the half-light,' said Hunter as they scrambled towards the tower.

'What, you'd rather we vandalised National Trust property in broad daylight?' said Sheldon.

'I would rather we weren't vandalising National Trust property at any time,' puffed Sicknote, who even in the gathering gloom appeared to be more than a little green.

'Look, we've been through this,' urged Smithies. 'We're not going to damage the building. We're not going to hurt anything or anyone. We're just taking a closer look at the tower and the way to do that's in the twilight. When *we* can't be seen.'

'Agreed!' said Tusia. 'So who's doing the climbing?'

'You. Obviously,' said Brodie.

'Me?'

'Oh, come on. When I first met you, you were climbing on the roof at Bletchley. This'll be a walk in the park for you!'

Tusia was obviously trying not to look too flattered. 'I'm not sure. It's a challenging incline. I mean, there'll be few footholds. It's not like the Bletchley roof where I had the—'

'Oh, for goodness' sake, Toots. If you don't think you can manage then I'm sure one of us boys can give it a go.'

Brodie had never seen Tusia move so fast.

They'd planned most of the operation at the bed and breakfast, leaving only the selection of climber till the arrival at the tower. Brodie noticed, as they harnessed Tusia to the ropes they'd brought, no one seemed to argue about her being the best one to go. Smithies insisted on giving her a safety talk though, and checking the fastening of the ropes several times.

'OK,' said Hunter, taking charge once it was clear he'd be keeping his feet firmly on the ground. 'You know what you're looking for?'

Tusia nodded and the torch they'd strapped to a band around her head wobbled, casting a flickering beam on the dewy grass.

'So you call back to us all the details and we check against the chart we've made.'

Tusia nodded again.

'And you try and keep your head still so you don't lose the torch.'

Tusia pulled a face.

'Oh, I really don't think I can bear to watch,' said Sicknote, steadying himself against the doorway to the tower. 'It's the River Wye all over again.' Another glare from Tusia made it clear he should have kept his comments to himself. 'Sorry, Tusia. So sorry. Absolutely sure you'll be totally fine.'

Tusia checked the fixing on the rope then began to climb.

The tower didn't offer many footholds. Scaling up from the windowsill to the porch across the door seemed to take forever. Kitty and Sheldon held the end of the rope between them while Hunter shouted instructions. Brodie took it from the comments shouted back that not all of his advice was entirely helpful.

'You're doing great, Tusia,' yelled Brodie.

'I know I am,' she called back. 'None of you'd even manage to get on to the porch.'

Brodie thought it might knock her confidence to argue. She looked up and Tusia was balanced

214

precariously on the pitched sloping roof of the porchway.

'OK, now you need to get on to the first-floor windowsill,' encouraged Kitty.

Tusia was standing with her arms spread-eagled along the wall of the tower, her feet balanced either side of the pitched ridge of the porch.

'It's a little tricky to move,' she called down.

'You need to step to the left. Can you see where your feet are?'

'No. Not entirely.'

Sicknote's groans were highly audible.

'OK, we'll talk you through,' said Brodie, pressing her hands together. 'Reach out with your left foot. Sort of sidestep.'

Tusia moved her foot and waved it precariously in the air.

Sicknote reached for his inhaler.

'OK. That's brilliant, Toots. A little further.'

Tusia's foot reached the windowsill. 'D'you think it will take her weight?' whispered Sheldon, tightening his grasp on the rope. 'Wood looks a bit rotten to me.'

'I can hear you,' called Tusia. 'And you're not helping.'

Sheldon grimaced apologetically.

'Oh, I can't watch,' said Sicknote.

Brodie tried to keep focused. 'You're doing great, Tusia. Nice and steady.'

She looked like a starfish, flung on to the side of the building. One foot on the porch, one on the windowsill, and her fingers scratching for a hold. 'Nice and steady,' Brodie said again.

'There's nothing nice about this,' Tusia called, finally launching her weight on to the sill. There was a rumbling sound from the porch. A slate skittered free and fell to the ground. The smash echoed around the air, broken only by the sound of more gulps on the inhaler.

'OK. Now where?' called Tusia.

Brodie squinted to see more clearly. 'Along and up to the top of the rounded tower. Can you manage that?'

'A walk in the park, you said,' she called. 'Some scary park.'

Brodie's throat was drying. She tried to swallow but the muscles in her neck seemed to have stopped working.

Tusia stood where she was, a cross against the window, then she moved to the side.

It happened so quickly there wasn't time to shout or call out.

Tusia's foot slipped. Her arms reeled, her body bounced against the window.

Sheldon and Kitty pulled tight on the rope.

'Tusia!' The scream split the air.

'It's OK. It's OK.'

'I think this is very far from OK. I think we should get her down. I think—'

Sicknote didn't get to finish his statement. The momentum of her slip thrust Tusia towards the rounded tower and she lurched on to the rounded roof.

'Tusia? You all right?' Brodie could hear the panic in her own voice.

'I've been better.'

'Haven't we all?' gulped Sicknote.

Tusia was crouching now, her knees bent so she was balanced on top of the rounded roof section of the tower side. 'Now where?'

'Can you make it on to the actual roof?' asked Brodie. 'If you look down from there, things might be easier.'

Tusia made a snorting noise. 'Easy, you say.'

'Easier,' corrected Brodie.

Brodie could hear Tusia breathing in deeply. Then she reached up and latched her fingers over the guttering of the roof.

'Can you haul yourself up?' called Hunter.

'Hey. Less of the hauling,' she snapped back.

Hunter rolled his eyes. 'I think I prefer her when she's about to fall,' he whispered.

Brodie pretended not to hear.

Tusia locked her fingers over the guttering and strained her arms to pull herself up on to the octagonal roof.

'Perfect,' yelled Brodie. 'You've done it.'

Tusia staggered for a moment, her body swaying a little in the breeze.

'What's she doing?' yelped Smithies. 'Don't stand there! Get sat down so you're steady.'

'But it's an amazing view from here. Honestly, you should see it.'

Granddad winced. 'Remember why you're up there!'

Tusia stopped wobbling and lowered herself down to crouch on the roof and then, turning so she faced out towards them, she lay down and peered over the edge of the tower. 'OK, troops. What am I looking for?'

'Are there any pictures under the paint?' called up Brodie.

Tusia peered closely, running the fingers of one hand across the flaking surface. 'There's definitely something. Looks like some sort of mythic character. He's flying.'

Four Great Winds – the Anemoi

East wind

North wind

west wind

South wind

'OK. Flying's good,' said Brodie. 'He could be one of the winds. That makes sense. Describe him.'

Tusia ran her hand across the paint again. 'He's very faint. But I'm pretty sure he's got a beard.'

Mr Bray rummaged in the bag and took out the chart Tusia had sketched earlier from the reference book. It showed the four winds usually included in the frieze work round a Tower of the Winds.

'OK. Beard's good. Can't be the South or East Wind then,' called up Mr Bray.

'But I'm on the east side, aren't I?' Tusia shouted down.

Hunter checked the compass he'd brought. 'She is.'

'Have I ever been wrong about direction before?' she called.

'No,' said Hunter reluctantly. 'So perhaps you're wrong about the beard.'

'I'm not wrong about the beard,' Tusia hissed.

'OK,' said Brodie, deciding the two of them having an argument when one of them was metres up in the air was probably not the best idea. 'What about if you move round and look at another side?' she suggested. 'Maybe the painters got it wrong and that's why they covered over the pictures.'

Tusia crawled around the octagonal roof on her stomach and positioned herself so she could see another of the hidden pictures. 'It's the same,' she called.

'What, this guy has a beard too?' called up Brodie.

'No. It's exactly the same guy. He has a beard and he's holding some sort of horn, just like the picture round there.'

Brodie looked down at the chart. 'Boreas, then.'

'What?'

'The North Wind,' said Brodie. 'That picture sounds like the one you sketched of the North Wind. But why are there two the same?'

'Not two,' called down Tusia, who'd begun to crawl round the tower again.

'They're not the same?' Brodie was getting frustrated.

'No. Well, yes. They are. And there's three of them.'

'Three of them?'

Tusia was moving again. 'No, make that four.'

'There are four pictures the same?'

'Yes. Four identical pictures.'

'So they did paint over them because they'd made a mistake, then,' said Kitty.

'Some ridiculous mistake,' said Hunter. 'I mean, why would you paint the same image four times?'

Brodie rubbed her face. 'You wouldn't do it as a mistake, would you? Not four times.'

'So perhaps that little quartet of pictures is trying to let us know that image is the most important,' suggested Sicknote.

'What, the North Wind's more important than the others?' asked Sheldon. 'Why's that?'

Brodie looked across at Smithies. 'Well, sir? Any ideas?'

Smithies lifted his glasses to his forehead. 'North Wind. Important, I guess. Yes. But more important than the others? I don't know.'

'There must be something, sir. Some myth or legend maybe?'

'And you haven't heard of it?' said Hunter.

'I don't know every story in the whole world, Hunter. I just thought, maybe . . .'

221

The rope attached to Tusia sagged a little in the middle.

'There's Hyperborea?' mumbled Smithies. 'It's a place. Somewhere beyond the North Wind. A really fabulous place.' He was obviously trying desperately to remember the details, his glasses balanced precariously on his forehead. 'There was this poem. Went something like

> *Never the Muse is absent*
> *from their ways: lyres clash and flutes cry*
> *and everywhere maiden choruses whirling.*
> *Neither disease nor bitter old age is mixed*
> *in their sacred blood; far from labour and battle*
> *they live.'*

'That's about somewhere called Hyperborea?' said Brodie. 'Sounds to me like a sort of perfect place if there's no disease or battle.'

'Like Avalon, then,' suggested Sheldon. 'All the clues we've found seem to lead to the same answer – Avalon. Different names for the same wonderful place.'

'Wonderful, yes. But we still haven't got a clue where this place is, or how to get there,' said Kitty.

Hunter twisted the end of the rope around his hand. 'So we have to keep working. Looking for more clues.

This just helps us know what we're looking for, doesn't it, sir?'

'Sorry? What?'

'Avalon, sir?' said Hunter. 'All these clues. If we just keep looking we're going to find out how to get there eventually, aren't we?'

Smithies looked a little ill. 'We keep looking, Hunter. Yes. That's what we do.'

'Sir, is there something you're not telling us?'

Smithies took his glasses from his forehead and slipped them into his pocket. 'The story of Hyperborea. There's some details.'

'Well, go on then,' called Tusia from the top of the tower.

'The story isn't that cheery about the hopes of finding this special place.'

'What's it say, then?'

Smithies pinched the bridge of his nose and began to recite.

> *'neither by ship nor on foot would you find*
> *the marvellous road to the assembly of the*
> *Hyperboreans.'*

'Well, that can't be right,' said Hunter. 'We think people *did* find Avalon.'

'That's what we think. But—'

'But nothing. We can't get all worried now.'

'I'm not worrying, Hunter,' Smithies said sharply. 'I'm being realistic. All the clues suggest Avalon's going to be really difficult to find.'

'But we're good at difficult! That's what we do. And perhaps there's a map. If the place is so hard to get to, then maybe someone made a map. Makes sense, doesn't it?'

'Perhaps,' said Smithies.

'So we just have to hope someone did,' said Hunter. 'We can't start thinking this is impossible. We can't leave here thinking that.'

'Actually, I'd rather you didn't leave till you got me down,' called Tusia.

Hunter tugged on the rope. 'No probs, Toots. But we have to get our heads round this first. Remember the Shepherd's Monument.'

'We're supposed to be encouraged by a monument?' said Sicknote.

'No,' said Hunter calmly. 'But by the fact that all the clues we've found here suggest the place is worth finding. And by the possibility that the person commemorated by that sculpture has been to where we want to go!'

* * *

'So where d'we go from here?' asked Sheldon. 'Seems like we might need to start looking for a map to help us find our way to Avalon, don't you think?'

They were back at the bed and breakfast and Hunter had just made off to the kitchen to see if he could rustle up the night-time adventurers any food. Mrs Hummel had said they should treat the place as their home and Hunter, at least, was taking her entirely at her word.

'Finding a map would be fantastic,' said Brodie. 'Where d'we start looking though?'

'Pictures,' suggested Tusia. 'We've covered most things on Jaeger's list of things to look for: quartets, poems and green fields. That leaves "pictures" and a map's like a picture.'

'Yeah. Get that,' said Hunter, re-entering the room with a plate full of sandwiches. 'You reckon a map to Avalon's going to be in one of the pictures round Shugborough Hall? Didn't we look at them all on our tour?'

Tusia reached for a salad sandwich and peeled it open to check there was no meat. 'Most of the pictures on the wall, yes. But there might be other pictures we haven't seen.'

'Why'd you say that, Toots?'

'The Lady Anson picture. The one where she was

wearing the ring. We haven't seen that actual painting, have we? Just a copy in a book.'

'You reckon that painting's got a hidden map in it?' said Hunter through a mouthful of sandwich.

'I don't know. Probably not. But I'm just saying, it was an important picture and it's odd we haven't seen it anywhere in the house, isn't it?'

'Why?'

'Because it was of Lady Anson! I sort of thought the family would want to keep it.'

'It's a big house. We could have missed it,' said Smithies. 'But I think that decides things, then. Gives us a plan. Tomorrow we ask Mrs Hummel where the painting of Lady Anson is.'

'We saw it in a book,' said Tusia, hurrying behind Mrs Hummel, who seemed more than a little irritated the team were still around and as yet there'd been no sign of any TV cameras. 'Lady Anson was holding a rolled-up sketch. We just wondered where in the house this particular painting is.'

Mrs Hummel stopped walking. 'Not everything you see in books still exists,' she said.

'Guess she hasn't ever heard the theory about Avalon, then,' whispered Brodie.

'But it's an incredible painting. Must have been a

family heirloom. Surely it's somewhere in the house.'

'I'm afraid not,' said Mrs Hummel. 'Some members of the family were not as cautious with their family heirlooms as they should have been.' She steered the team into the verandah room behind the library and shut the door. 'Look, this family isn't without its money worries, you know. Times get hard for everyone. Why else would this fabulous home be open to allow members of the public to troop through its doors? In the early 1800s the Anson family hit a little bit of financial trouble. Servants were laid off and left the estate, various treasures from the house were removed or passed on and then, in 1842, there was something called the Great Anson Sale.'

'Things from here were sold?' said Brodie.

'Oh yes. Lots of incredibly important pieces. Every book in the library in fact, bar one, and the family documents.'

'But we've been using books in the library,' said Kitty.

'Replacements of the original stock,' explained Mrs Hummel. 'George Anson II, who was head of the family then, saw selling as the only way to settle his debts. We've tried to restock but of course we haven't got everything back. The picture of Lady Anson you mentioned was sold to the Duke of Devonshire.'

'What about the ring that Lady Anson wore in the picture?' whispered Sheldon. 'Shouldn't we be tracking that down too? We should ask about the ring.'

Smithies stepped forward towards Mrs Hummel and smiled warmly. 'You've been very helpful,' he said. 'And it seems mean to press on your good nature any further. It's just, I wonder if there's any records of the sales?'

'Of course.'

'And could we take a look at them?' pressed Smithies.

Mrs Hummel hesitated.

'For the sake of historical accuracy,' he added with a wink.

Mrs Hummel weakened. 'I can find them for you and bring them through to the library,' she said. 'If it would be helpful.'

16

Coin of Death

'At last, you've finally given me something to do with numbers,' grinned Hunter, tucking a pencil behind his ear and tapping on the pages of the ledger Mrs Hummel had brought them. 'Did you know the value of a guinea used to fluctuate with the price of gold and so prices in the 1800s are hard to calculate with total accuracy?'

'I didn't know that,' said Tusia in a voice forced through her teeth, making it sound very much as if she didn't know and didn't really care much either.

'These Ansons must have been in a right mess with money. Thomas, 2nd Viscount Anson, had a huge gambling debt. They really did sell everything they could.' Hunter gazed intently at the ledger. 'And here it is,' he said, prodding the page with his finger so the pencil wobbled behind his ear. 'Sale of the painting of Lady Anson to the Duke of Devonshire.'

'I've found some details about him,' called Tusia from the far end of the room, where she was flicking through the pages of an aristocracy Who's Who book. 'He lived down the road at the time, but he also had homes in Sussex, by the sea. But here's the best bit.' She waited for everyone to turn to face her. 'Where d'you think William Cavendish 7th Duke of Devonshire went to university?'

'Tell me it was Cambridge,' Brodie said nervously.

'Certainly was. That connection might be important.'

'But did he buy the ring?' asked Sheldon tentatively.

Hunter raised his head from looking at the ledger. 'No.'

'You sure?' said Tusia sullenly.

'Absolutely sure. No rings were sold to the Duke. But there's a reference to a ring here. Not bought by anyone from Cambridge though. This guy was American. Someone called William Blackhouse Astor Jr.'

'Heard of him,' said Sicknote. 'The Astors were loaded. Millionaires probably. Billionaires even.'

'Very nice for them. But how d'we know this Astor guy bought the ring from the picture?' asked Brodie. 'A ring like the one worn by the Knights of Neustria?'

'We don't,' said Hunter. 'But it's the only ring and it's listed just after the portrait in the listing. The other stuff listed is all books.'

Smithies leant over his shoulder to get a closer look.

'D'you know any of this lot, sir? Maybe some of them had clues about Avalon and because they were sold we'll never know.'

Smithies scanned the list. 'Newton's *Chronology of Ancient Kingdoms Amended.*'

'Sounds like that one might have stuff in it about Avalon,' Brodie offered.

'No making leaps, Brodie. But this might be important. It mentions books by Rousseau. That's interesting.'

Sheldon made a face at Hunter. 'Really? That's interesting?'

'Oscar. D'you want to explain the importance of Rousseau to them?'

'Absolutely. Jean Jacques Rousseau was born in Geneva in the early 1700s and he wrote about how it was important to educate the whole person. He believed all people were born equal, and that got him into a lot of trouble.'

'What kind of trouble?'

'The kind that got your books burned,' explained Sicknote.

'Well, that's great,' said Tusia. She saw Brodie's face and quickly added, 'What I mean is, that all fits with the idea of hiding truth and books surviving fire, doesn't it? I wonder why his books were so important to the Ansons?'

'Oh, I know,' said Sicknote, rising from his chair. 'This is brilliant. And crazy. Rousseau wrote a book called *Emile* and I'd never made the connection before. But the hero was called Anson and he travelled round the world taking the child Emile to uninhabited lands and islands.'

'Another link to Avalon?' asked Brodie.

'Could be,' said Sicknote.

'So maybe the story in the novel's really a true story,' said Sheldon. 'And maybe instead of a made-up person called Emile who got to see Avalon, the real child was Renata, the girl the Shepherd's Monument was for.'

The air was bristling with energy. Brodie's ears were burning.

'Hold on.' Tusia had her hand in the air. 'That's a great connection. But we had to know about the story Rousseau wrote to understand that link. But what about the book itself?'

'Toots?'

'Mrs Hummel said all except one of the books were sold in the sale, right?'

'All except one,' confirmed Hunter. 'These books in the library are just replacements bought later.'

'So if all the books except one were sold,' said Tusia, 'and we could still work out clues from just the list of the books that were here, then the single book that wasn't sold must be *really* important. Agreed?'

There was a general ripple of agreement.

'The single book that wasn't got rid of when all the others were must be vital for us to *actually see*, not just know about. It must be so special a replacement of it wouldn't do. There must be something important about the actual copy of the book left behind.'

Another ripple of agreement.

'So we need to find that book,' said Brodie.

The room was filled with silence.

'Well, Hunter?'

Hunter was flicking through the pages of the sales ledger.

'Anytime you could let us know which book it was would be great.'

'I'm on it. I'm on it,' he snapped. He looked up and he read the words written in copperplate writing at the bottom of the page:

The only book to be held back from the 1842 sale, perhaps as a single representative example of

Thomas Anson's collection, was a copy of the French translation of JJ Winckelmann's 'Letter about the Herculanean Discoveries of 1762'.

Kerrith lifted her blood-red nails from the computer keys and stared at the screen. The Director had been insistent about finding the answers in the history books. Kerrith had little time for history. She also had little time for books. But she'd been intrigued. Made curious enough by his suggestion to do some research. And the answers to that research provided exciting reading.

1912 and 1952. The search had been relatively easy. The answers shocking.

She pushed back in her chair and linked her hands behind her head. Disaster and darkness. That's what the Director had told her to look for.

Now she knew what he'd been talking about. 1,490 deaths in 1912 and 12,000 in 1952. All that to cause a diversion?

She pressed 'print' and waited for the newspaper articles to churn from the printer. The sinking of the great liner *Titanic*, and the forming of a great fog in the centre of London. Both terrible disasters, but how could those in power have been involved? Surely they were just accidents. Both of them. Weren't they?

Kerrith put the articles on the desk then tapped the

keyboard with her nail, scrolling the cursor across the date icon. 2013. Sixty-one years since the darkness. One hundred and one years since the disaster. One hundred and one years since the finding of MS 408. She felt her stomach clench with nerves. The Director liked the notion of anniversaries. And the thought didn't scare her. It thrilled her.

'It has to be here.' Brodie was running her fingers along the spines of the books, making it look like she was playing a harp.

'There's just an awfully big lot of "here", here,' said Kitty, before lowering her head and trying to look like she was concentrating.

'And it doesn't sound like the most inspiring of reads, anyway,' said Sheldon, making his own fingers drum loudly and rhythmically on the spines.

Brodie shook her head in exasperation. 'Tusia's right. I don't think this will be about the story in the book,' she said, never lifting her eyes from the search. 'It's got to be something about the physical copy. When the Ansons were paying off Thomas's gambling debts they kept just this book and that seems too weird unless the actual thing is important.'

Tusia called up from her position on her knees at the lowest shelves. 'It must be something about how the books looks or feels.'

'Or the number of pages,' said Hunter.

'Or the pictures inside,' added Kitty.

'I've got it!' Brodie yelled suddenly. 'Winckelmann's "Letter about the Herculanean Discoveries of 1762".'

She pulled the tiny volume from the shelf. It was bound in red leather. Golden letters were embossed on the spine. And it was heavy. Heavier than it should have been. Too heavy.

Brodie looked up. She passed the book to Tusia and then waited for her friend to register surprise.

'Well,' said Brodie. 'You feel it too?'

Tusia nodded.

'Feel what?' asked Hunter, leaning forward for a closer look. 'Is it made of chocolate or something?'

'It's heavy.'

'Well, some book about Herculanean discoveries two hundred and fifty years ago was hardly going to be light reading, was it?' snorted Sheldon. 'I mean, I expect it's full of all sorts of words we don't understand and—'

'I mean it weighs a lot.'

'Oh.'

'Too much for such a little book.'

'Oh.'

'Which must mean there's something hidden inside.

Probably in the cover,' said Tusia, opening her eyes wide. 'What d'you think?'

'Well, I think the chances of you being right are fairly high if you say it's particularly heavy,' went on Sicknote.

'No. I mean, what d'you think we should do to get inside the cover?'

'Oh, please.' Sicknote slumped down on to the nearest seat and put his head in his hands. 'It's Sir Francis Bacon's ring all over again. Why is it you lot are so keen to destroy things?'

'Not destroy,' said Hunter. 'Just look inside for answers.'

'Oh, this should be good,' said Kitty, rubbing her hands together. 'What're you going to do? Rip it open page by page?'

Brodie felt a shiver run across her skin. 'There'll be no ripping,' she insisted, stepping forward.

Tusia held the book and the light from the mirrored bookcase ends danced on the cover.

It was then Brodie knew what she should do.

'I'm ready,' she said, taking the book from Tusia. 'Are you?'

The mirror Brodie had got for her birthday was small and light. The edges encircled by a silver frame. The mirror had already provided answers. Now was its moment to shine again.

She didn't have to explain to Tusia what she should do. Her friend had read her mind. She took the mirror from Brodie and peeled back the silver casing to reveal the sharp and naked edge of the polished glass.

'Oh, this can't be good,' moaned Sicknote, who'd lifted his eyes momentarily to look across the room. 'Seriously, this can't be good.'

'It's necessary,' said Brodie, taking the skinned mirror from Tusia and flicking the front cover of the book open. 'Ready?' she said again. This time there was a mumble of agreement.

The unsheathed mirror worked as a blade. It sliced through the leather. The cover of the book opened like an envelope. And out fell a sheath of paper and a heavy golden disc.

'It's a coin,' said Hunter, reaching down to retrieve it from the floor. 'You had to throw coins into that Trevi Fountain in Rome you told us about, B. Remember? The fountain of true love which gave us the connection with Lucia and her daughter Renata. D'you think that's why it's there?'

'Not sure,' said Brodie. 'But we've got a piece of paper and a coin. Maybe they're more messages left behind by the Knights?'

238

* * *

Hunter twisted the golden coin in and out of his fingers like a poker player at Monte Carlo toying with a betting chip.

'You should be careful with that,' said Tusia. 'It's a clue.'

'It's a coin,' said Hunter. 'What can I possibly do to damage a coin?'

It slipped, at that moment, from between his fingers, rolled across the floor and bounced against the skirting board.

They'd taken their research back to the only cyber café in Great Haywood because they all had the distinct feeling people at Shugborough Hall were getting a little tired of them. Besides, they were sure none of the books in the Shugborough library had the information they needed and so a more modern form of research was called for. They wanted information about the coin.

The folded piece of paper which had fallen from the back cover of the book was easy to identify. A copy of the American Declaration of Independence.

Why a copy of a document written mainly by Thomas Jefferson and adopted by America's Congress in 1776 had been folded up and placed inside the cover of the book was a puzzle to them, but at least Sicknote knew lots about the document.

'Thomas Jefferson was a great man,' Sicknote said on more than one occasion as they'd travelled back to the village in the Matroyska. 'You've got to love what he said.' He quoted great chunks of the Declaration to them.

'*We hold these truths to be self-evident, that all men are created equal; that they are endowed by their Creator with inherent and inalienable Rights; that among these, are Life, Liberty, and the pursuit of Happiness . . .*'

'Got to give it to old TJ,' said Hunter. 'He knew what he was talking about.'

Sheldon laughed. 'TJ. D'you really have to give everyone a nickname?'

'Thomas Jefferson's such a mouthful.'

Tusia was looking thoughtful. 'I've heard that name before.'

'Yeah. The writer of the Declaration! Keep up, Toots.'

'No. Somewhere else. Back at Shugborough. I can't think—'

'The servant?' said Kitty. 'The guy who went back to Rome with Lucia Narora, remember!'

'Yes! Thomas Jefferson Beale. That can't be coincidence, can it?' said Tusia. 'We've got to remember that connection surely!'

Brodie made a note of it in the logbook.

Thomas Jefferson Beale

↓
US President

↓
Shugborough Servant

'Great,' said Hunter. 'A possible connection between a hidden document we found and someone who worked for the Ansons. But what about this coin? This has got to be the puzzler.'

The coin was larger than most and one side showed the head of a fairly old and portly man. The words 'JOHN FULLER esq ROSE HILL SUSSEX' were written around the edge and, on the back of the coin, the years the man had been born and died.

'It's a funeral medallion,' explained Smithies. 'Certain people had them made to be given out to mourners at their funerals as mementos.'

'So you'd have to know your date of death in advance, then,' mused Kitty, wrinkling her forehead in confusion.

Smithies smiled at her supportively. 'I think they added that bit when you actually died,' he said. 'Seems the most logical way to go about it.'

Kitty looked very relieved.

'So who was this John Fuller, then?' asked Sheldon. 'And what's his connection with the American Declaration of Independence? And why were these things left behind for us to find?'

Tusia turned away from the computer screen to face them. 'No idea about the Declaration. But as for John Fuller . . .' She waited to give her words impact. 'He was a madman.'

An expectant silence hung on the air.

'No, really,' said Tusia, turning back to face the screen. 'According to what I can find on the Internet, he really was mad. The name Jack's used sometimes instead of John and they called him Mad Jack Fuller. Surely you couldn't get clearer than that?'

Hunter laughed and spun the coin once more in his fingers. 'Was he mad like Levitov and Newbold were said to be?'

Kitty's face was crumpled and confused again.

'Levitov and Newbold were two guys who tried to read MS 408,' Hunter explained. 'The authorities declared they were mad.'

'The authorities tend to do that with people who seem to get close to finding answers about the manuscript. Maybe Fuller was investigating MS 408. And maybe he got near to finding answers,' he said. 'That could be the reason they called him Mad Jack.'

'Or he could just have been mad,' said Tusia, bringing them back to earth rather quickly.

'So what else do we know about him?' asked Sheldon, moving forward so he could see the screen.

Tusia read aloud for the benefit of the others. 'Fuller was born in 1757 and in 1780 he was elected MP. He served in parliament for a while which could be where he met George Anson II who was also an MP. That's our Anson . . . of Shugborough Hall.'

'OK. There's a link to Shugborough. Anything else?' asked Brodie.

'Not really. He wasn't a poet. He wasn't a musician. And he didn't go to Cambridge University. No links there.'

'What did he do?'

'Built things. It says he liked to give local workmen the chance of a job,' she explained. 'Apparently, he had this wooden lighthouse built on cliffs at Beachy Head in Eastbourne. Later, in 1832, they built a permanent lighthouse there called the Belle Toute Lighthouse. But he built loads of other things too.'

'Monuments and secret coded statues?' asked Sheldon.

'Maybe.'

Hunter put the coin down on the table. 'And this Rose Hill? That was his home?' he asked, peering again

Mad 'Jack' Fuller

Say what you mean!

Born in 1757
↓
Elected MP in 1780 → Met George Anson
↓
Built things!
↓
Beachy Head Lighthouse
↓
became Belle Toute Lighthouse

Lived at Rose Hill → became Brightling Park

at the face of the coin.

Tusia nodded. 'Although it changed its name to Brightling Park.'

'So do you think we should try and find the place where this Fuller is buried, then?' Smithies asked tentatively. 'We've found a funeral medallion. Seems to me we should check out his grave. Graves have been kind of helpful so far. Fuller's grave might have a message like the Shepherd's Monument.'

There was a rumble of agreement.

'And we should just leave Shugborough? Not explain to Mrs Hummel why we're moving on?'

'I can do that,' said Granddad. 'Stay a while and explain we've got to take our research elsewhere. It'll give me time to settle the bill for the bed and breakfast, make contact with Fabyan and Tandi again and catch them up with what we know and,' he seemed embarrassed by the next bit, 'catch up with myself a bit.'

'All our speed is wearing you out?' asked Smithies sympathetically.

Granddad shook his head, but Brodie wasn't entirely sure he was being honest. 'Not really. I've just got to thinking about how much we're finding out about hidden truths and there's a few things I need to sort while I can.'

'But you'll be all right, Granddad?' Brodie knew her question sounded more like she was pleading. 'You'll catch up with us when we've found out more?'

Mr Bray clutched her hands tightly. 'I'll be right behind you,' he said in little more than a whisper. 'Just like I always am.'

The Pyramid Tomb

It felt good to be back on the road again. Good to be heading away from Shugborough with new clues and a new direction. It seemed a little uncomfortable that they were heading off to a grave site once more but this did seem to be the pattern of things. Answers seemed to be more clearly hidden at the point of death. There was nothing left to lose by then.

Brodie leant her head against the window as the Matroyska pulled its way towards Brightling. It was nice to be back in Sussex again. And reassuring to hear the sound of Kitty's motorbike roaring behind them. Not so comforting was the sound of sputtering and the large cloud of black smoke filling the air as they left the town of Lewes and headed towards Eastbourne.

'We'll have to pull over,' groaned Tusia. 'The carbon Kitty's bike is belching into the air will take weeks to neutralise.'

Hunter pulled a face. 'I was hoping we'd stop for food,' he muttered, 'whatever the carbon costs. *I'll* be neutralised if I don't eat soon.'

Brodie tried to bat away the chance of a row by pointing out a small takeaway van at the side of the road and Sheldon waved wildly from the window, gesturing to Kitty that they were about to stop. Kitty wasn't happy. She spent ages running her hands over the bodywork of the bike and only when she'd pulled away several bits of twig and debris which must have caught in the undercarriage and be causing the problem did she agree to join them for a sandwich.

'Who do you suppose that guy is?' Kitty asked, sinking down to sit on the grass alongside them and reaching for a chicken mayo butty. 'Looks kind of weird.'

Brodie followed Kitty's line of gaze up on to the hill behind them where a huge chalk figure of a man had been carved into the grass.

'Woman making the butties told me he's called the Long Man of Wilmington,' said Hunter through a mouthful of cheese and pickle.

'Apparently he was carved on the hillside in

1512-ish. So he's seriously old,' added Sheldon.

Brodie narrowed her eyes to see more clearly while Hunter sputtered on his sandwich. '1512 makes him about the same age as MS 408,' he said. 'Weird, isn't it? That things can last that long. Things we don't understand, like huge chalk men carved on hillsides and books no one can read.'

The rest of the group turned to look at the chalked figure on the hillside.

'I like it,' said Tusia. 'A sign in a "green field" like Jaeger told us to look for.'

'And in the part of the world where the very first clue was hidden,' added Smithies.

The rest of the team looked along the line. 'The Firebird Code,' he explained. 'Hidden in the Royal Pavilion. Brighton. Sussex. Remember?'

Hunter munched on his sandwich. 'I just hope Mad Jack Fuller's grave is ready for us,' he announced. 'Now we're tuned in, we're finding signs and symbols everywhere.'

Brodie smiled and reached for her mobile. She wanted to ring her granddad. Now seemed like a good time to talk.

'We have a problem, ma'am.'

Kerrith looked up from her desk and put down the

pages she'd been scrutinising. 'Go on.'

The young man in the doorway stepped awkwardly from one foot to the other.

'I'm waiting.'

'There's been a breakdown in the tracking device,' he said, his hands still firmly locked together. 'On the girl's motorbike. We seem to have lost function.'

'They're no longer in Staffordshire?'

'No, ma'am. They moved on this morning. Seemed to be making for the south coast and then there was a fault in the tracker.'

Kerrith bunched her hands into fists.

'We have intercepted two mobile phone calls though.' He offered these words like a child begging for extra sweets.

'And the nature of these calls?'

The young man withdrew a clipboard tucked under his arm and began to scan his notes. 'The first concerned the young Bray girl. She rang her grandfather.'

'He's no longer with them?'

'No, ma'am.' He glanced again at his notes. 'There was some friendly discussion and then some reference to someone called Jack Fuller.' The man waited to see if the name registered surprise or recognition. Kerrith's face showed neither. 'I'm afraid it was difficult to follow, although I have the transcript here.'

'And the other call?'

'Between the old man and Tandari,' he said with more enthusiasm.

Kerrith leant back on her chair.

'Seems she's still with the American, but the old man was asking her advice. Wanting her to bring something from Bletchley for the child to see. Wondered if the time was right.'

Kerrith licked the tips of her fingers and smoothed them along her eyebrows.

'Will that be all, ma'am?'

Kerrith waited. 'One other thing,' she said, lowering her hands to her desk. 'The Director. Is he in the building?'

'Yes.'

'Arrange a meeting,' she said. 'I need to see him today.'

Tusia held the printout from the Route Planner service at the cyber café and barked directions loudly as Smithies steered the Matroyska down some seriously narrow country lanes. She had to resort to this because Sheldon was playing his harmonica while everyone else sang a rousing sea shanty. Sicknote had taken to draping his head in a blanket and was mumbling about flashing lights on his retinas and the approach of a migraine.

What Brodie hoped they were in fact approaching was the church of St Thomas à Becket, Brightling, where Mad Jack Fuller had been buried.

'Here,' squealed Tusia, banging the dashboard like a driving examiner signalling for an emergency stop. Smithies slammed on the brakes and the Matroyska sputtered to a halt, Kitty's motorbike drawing to a stop beside them.

The church was poised on top of a hill and a valley lined by a stout brick wall stretched into the distance.

'Fuller had the wall built, apparently,' said Tusia, reading from the notes they'd printed. 'Bit odd to have walls here just to go round fields. Most farmers had hedges. But Fuller said building walls gave locals a job.'

It was getting cold and a slight drizzle was beginning to fall as Smithies led the way towards the entrance to St Thomas à Becket churchyard.

'OK,' said Smithies, drawing the team to order. 'We need to split up and try and find his gravestone.'

'Erm, Smithies.'

'Plan is to look around the churchyard and find the stone. Then look for symbols or letters or signs on that stone which might be helpful.'

'Erm, sir?'

'And remember to be open-minded about what you find. The funeral medal's why we're here but we haven't got any idea yet where that clue's going to take us.'

'Sir.' Hunter was practically shouting.

'What is it, Hunter? I really don't think a place of worship in the middle of the English countryside is actually the place for shouting!' He growled in a voice which was, to be fair to Hunter, hardly quieter than the one the boy himself had used.

'Well, neither would a churchyard in a place of worship in the middle of the English countryside be a place for one of those,' Hunter said, waving behind him.

Brodie turned to look.

She had to agree Hunter had a point.

'It's a pyramid,' gasped Brodie, staggering forward across the churchyard. 'An actual, real, ginormous pyramid. In a churchyard. An English churchyard.'

'More to the point,' said Tusia, 'what's it doing here?'

She broke free of the group and led the way through the rain towards the lower left of the graveyard and the pyramid which appeared to be bursting from the ground. The dark-grey stone structure dwarfed the gravestones jutting like teeth from the damp grass around it.

'What in the name of Creme Egg filling is that?'

mumbled Hunter. 'I mean, forget Mad Jack Fuller's grave. This has got to be the maddest thing I've seen.'

Tusia called back to him over her shoulder. 'We shouldn't forget Mad Jack Fuller's grave,' she said.

'Are you sure, Toots, cos it's going to have to go a long way to beat this?'

Tusia scowled. 'It *is* this.'

'You what?'

'I said, it is this,' Tusia said again, slowly, as if speaking in a foreign language.

'It's what?'

Tusia folded her arms across her chest. 'This is the grave of Mad Jack Fuller,' she said. 'There's a sign here that says so.'

Hunter hurried forward. Brodie jogged to join him and then they stood, like guests waiting to be invited inside, in front of the doorway to the pyramid.

'Totally insane,' said Brodie, reading from the information sign. 'It says here, Fuller had the pyramid built before he died and when he was dead, they sat his body at a feasting table inside the pyramid.'

Hunter's eyes widened.

'Said he wanted to be well fed before he journeyed on.'

'He wasn't totally mad, then.'

'It says here,' added Sheldon, 'he asked to have

broken glass scattered at the entrance so if the devil or grave robbers came in the night they'd literally be stopped in their tracks.'

Brodie grimaced. 'Now, that's totally bonkers.' She skirted round the rest of the pyramid. 'Mad Jack Fuller. They got that right.'

'And we got it right,' said Tusia, her face taking on a pinkish glow which seemed to have little to do with the rain that was falling.

'How so?' asked Sicknote, who himself was looking a little peaky.

'The pyramid. It's perfect,' she said. 'Totally and utterly perfect.'

'It's mad, Toots, we'll give you that,' said Hunter. 'But perfect? Are you sure?'

Tusia hurried back to the Matroyska.

'Was it something I said?' asked Hunter.

Tusia returned, panting a little, and carrying the guidebook to Shugborough Hall. 'The Poussin picture. Of Arcadia,' gasped Tusia. 'Remember?'

She flicked to the page showing the Poussin sketch.

'And then the Shepherd's Monument version,' Tusia continued, struggling to catch her breath. 'Remember the difference?' She flicked again through the book.

'I remember,' said Hunter. 'The image was reversed.'

'And what else?' said Tusia. 'What else about it was different?'

'It was made of stone and not painted on paper,' said Sheldon.

'What else?' Tusia snapped the book open and thrust it between them. Then she jabbed at the page. And then everyone saw the difference she was trying to make them see.

A structure on top of the tomb in the picture. A pyramid.

'It doesn't matter how many times you look at it, B,' implored Hunter. 'Staring won't make it make sense.'

Brodie rubbed her eyes reluctantly. No single part of her wanted to admit he might be right.

They'd spent about an hour walking round and round the pyramid grave at St Thomas à Becket's churchyard. They'd scrutinised the pyramid from every angle. They'd counted the level of the bricks. They'd peered in the padlocked grille doorway. And then, when they were nearly about to give up, they'd found the inscription and written it down.

Paths of Glory lead but to the grave

Brodie was now peering, trying somehow to turn the words into something that pointed them onward. But all the words did was convince them they'd reached another dead end.

They sat in the Matroyska. The rain lashed against the window. And the meal from the local chip shop was a distant memory apart from the lingering smell of vinegar and battered cod.

'We can't really be sleeping in here tonight,' moaned Sicknote from his position near the back. 'My lumbago's playing up and I should be reclining in a bed with spring and elevation.'

'I'll give him spring and elevation,' whispered Hunter.

Smithies mumbled a reproach. 'I've explained this is simply a stopgap. When we've heard from Mr Bray and Tandi we'll be making a move. Our problem is we don't know yet where that move will be to. So we wait.'

'Seriously, B. You're making me nervous with all that staring. Just come and chill a moment and wait for the olds to give us a call, will you? With the power of the World Wide Web they should be able to fill in the gaps and help us out soon.'

'Gaps,' snorted Brodie. 'What about great gigantic holes? We've found a pyramid and so there has to be a connection to the clues we found at Shugborough but we're at a dead end!'

'It *is* a grave after all, Brodie,' chimed in Sheldon. 'Dead end. Grave. Get it?'

From the scowl flitting across Tusia's face, she wasn't amused. 'We've just got to think round the idea. Outside the box. And,' she said, 'we shouldn't ignore the other clues. It wasn't just the death medal we found, you know.'

Sheldon seized on this, keen to redeem himself. 'You're right. So let's think about all the other leads we've got.' He called down the length of the Matroyska. 'Kitty. You up for note taking?'

Kitty rummaged around to find the logbook and unloosened a pencil from Tusia's hair.

'OK,' said Hunter. 'All set.'

Smithies spoke first. 'The Declaration of Independence.' He allowed Kitty to write this down on a clean page. 'Thomas Jefferson's finest work. A statement of all men being equal. Why d'you think that was hidden in the only book left in the Anson library?'

'Because Avalon should be available for everyone?' suggested Tusia.

'I thought everyone in the Arthur myths was *chosen* to do things. Like taking the sword out of the stone?' offered Kitty.

'But wasn't there a round table for the knights?' said Tusia. 'Where no one was seen as more important than any other, even the king?'

'True,' said Brodie.

'And isn't Avalon where Arthur goes when he's injured anyway?' said Hunter, twisting the Fuller medallion again. 'Camelot's where he was king, but Avalon's where he goes when it's all over.'

'I like that idea,' said Brodie. 'Could be why the Declaration's there, then. Because Avalon is a place where everyone is equal.'

'Sounds good,' said Sheldon. 'What else are we missing?'

'The ring,' said Kitty. 'You said there was a ring worn by Lady Anson in the paintings and that this duke from Sussex bought the painting but some rich American guy bought the ring.'

'The Knights of Neustria ring,' said Brodie. 'Like the one worn by Coleridge and Bacon. We should have asked Fabyan about that when Tandi rang us. Who d'you say bought the ring?'

'Blackhouse Astor,' said Sheldon. 'And I did mention it to Fabyan when you let me speak to him on the phone. And it wasn't good news. I didn't say anything then. You were so fed up already.' Sheldon looked more than a little awkward. 'Fabyan knew about this

Blackhouse Astor guy. I was thinking one American billionaire might have heard of another one. Anyway, Fabyan said Blackhouse Astor had a son, John Jacob Astor IV, who inherited everything Blackhouse Astor owned.'

'Why didn't you tell us that?' asked Tusia. 'We've just got to find out what happened to this John Jacob Astor if we want to track down the ring.'

'Well, the thing is, the ring was listed as being in the possession of a John Jacob Astor who was a survivor on a rather famous ship.'

'More famous than the *Covadonga* which may have been to Avalon?' asked Kitty.

Sheldon nodded. 'You'll have heard of this ship. The RMS *Titanic*.'

'Wow. So this John Jacob Astor had the ring and he was a survivor from the *Titanic*?'

'That's the problem,' Sheldon went on. 'Fabyan says John Jacob Astor *didn't* survive when the *Titanic* sank. He drowned. The records must be wrong. So he can't have had the ring.' He was struggling to make sense. 'Fabyan said Astor had a son called Vincent and perhaps he inherited the ring. But Vincent wasn't a survivor from the *Titanic* so that sort of makes a mess of the story.'

'This just isn't fair,' Brodie moaned. 'Every time we

- Declaration of Independence
  - Thomas Jefferson's Work
  - All men are equal
    - Maybe in Avalon people are equal
  - Sword in stone V round table ...... K of N?
    - Lady Anson's ring
    - Bought by an American / Blackhouse Astor
  - John Jacob inherited everything
  - Survivor from Titanic
  - Drowned on Titanic

think we've got a clue it ends in a dead end.'

'*Paths of glory lead but to the grave,*' said Tusia. 'Kind of got to think that's true.'

'We've got nothing. Nothing at all. The trail's run cold.' Brodie twisted her fingers through the end of her hair as if trying to grab hold of an escaping thought that might just make some sense. 'We thought we'd worked out Avalon was really there. Maybe people have been there. Written about it and that's what MS 408 is. A book all about an incredible place. But it comes back to the unbreakable code. We still can't read a single word. How can we go on?'

18

Keeping Quiet
on the Ship of Dreams

'I'm most impressed, Miss Vernan. Seems you've done your research thoroughly.'

Kerrith felt a ripple of excitement. It always felt good to know the Director was happy with her work. 'I had a few questions, though, sir?' she said. 'If that's OK.'

The Director leant back on his chair. He scanned the pages she'd printed then put them aside and folded his arms. 'Fire away, Miss Vernan.'

'1912,' Kerrith began tentatively. 'About fifteen hundred lives were lost. And it was all part of a distraction?'

The Director looked a little annoyed. '1912 and

that busybody Voynich stumbled on his encrypted document. The world was waiting for a story. We couldn't be sure what the manuscript would say. We guessed it wouldn't fit with our plan of how we wanted things to be. So we did all we could to ensure the world got their story. But on our terms, you understand. Not perhaps the story Voynich wanted told, but one to draw minds away from his adventures.'

'But so many lives, sir?'

'Well, we had to be sure.'

'Sure, sir?'

'People like Voynich need money if they're going to find answers. That's why the involvement of that crackpot Fabyan with the work at Station X is so displeasing to me. Money buys you all sorts of openings. And there was one particular American billionaire who'd have opened many a door for young Voynich. He was the most wealthy casualty of the operation. In fact, the richest man in the world at the time.'

'And all the others, sir?'

The Director leant forward. 'You seem to think we're claiming total responsibility for the disaster of 1912, Miss Vernan.'

'Well, aren't you?'

The Director considered his answer. 'Not

responsibility. We just worked with the situation. We just allowed nature to take its course when we could have intervened.'

Kerrith looked down at her shoes. 'But what exactly did you do, sir? I mean, the *Titanic* sank because it hit an iceberg. Everybody knows that. What exactly did people here in the Black Chamber do to get involved?'

The Director turned his back on her and delved into a drawer in a tall filing cabinet in the corner, pulling out a folder and flicking through the pages as he spoke. 'Here,' he said, passing her a poor-quality Photostat. 'A careful reading of the history books will show you a mystery ship watched the sinking happen.'

Kerrith looked down at the page he'd offered her, drinking in the wording.

'It's a shame those on board the mystery ship didn't help,' he said. 'But, like I say, the world needed a distraction. They needed to believe nature and not man had allowed those deaths.'

Kerrith felt her skin prickle with excitement. 'And nature was part of the problem in 1952, sir?' pressed Kerrith.

A fragment of a new smile twitched across the Director's mouth. 'Weather conditions and lack of wind meant a terrible darkness cloaked our capital city between the 5th and the 9th of December of that year. But the situation may not have been so grave if those who were cold hadn't burnt contaminated coal.'

'The coal burning added to the deaths?'

'No one could blame people for wanting to be warm. We just went with a public need. Even we couldn't have predicted the terrible loss of life. But Friedman senior was instigating his Study Group in the early fifties and we had to send out a warning.' He lurched forward and banged the desk with the flat of his hand. 'You see, it's when the Americans and Europeans combine that we're at our most vulnerable. And that's what worries me now. We've allowed these has-beens and wannabes to toy with the manuscript and explore the myths and legends about its creation. But once they started involving others: since they began to leave Station X and spread their network of lies and deceit, I have felt less comfortable.'

'And so you'll plan a modern-day distraction, sir?' Kerrith asked slowly.

'We could. Or we could certainly take their minds off their research for a while.'

Kerrith waited.

'You want me to tell you, Miss Vernan?' the Director mocked. 'You want me to include you in the plans we've made?'

'I hoped you would.'

The Director leant back again and considered the idea. 'And you know if I include you, you'll be culpable. Implicated if anything should go wrong.'

Kerrith could feel her veins throbbing with adrenaline.

The Director sensed her excitement. 'We shall be following the model used in years gone by,' he said. 'A "natural" disaster that with hindsight could have been averted. But one which will, at the time, cause distress and chaos. So much chaos that for a while all media and press attention will be focused there. Then, under the cover of the distraction, we'll hit that annoying little team of has-beens where it really hurts.' His smile was broad now. 'I've been pondering their connection with Friedman. Seems to me, since our security surrounding him was breached, he's become a liability. I think he needs dealing with.'

'I don't quite understand.'

The Director ran his hand along his chin. 'For a while I've taken the operation in the wrong direction, Miss Vernan. I mistakenly believed taking a vital player from their team, and sharing the scandal of his involvement with the death of the girl's mother, would be enough to end their little game. Darkening the name of one of their own should have been sufficient. But I was wrong. Capturing Friedman and keeping him from them has simply served to strengthen the myth. Instead of rejecting him, the girl wants to understand him. Wants to know his side of the story. It seems our friends at Station X are obsessed with truth.' He spat the words as if they repulsed him. 'And if we end up with Friedman dying in captivity then we make a martyr of him. The determination of those has-beens to find an answer will grow and grow.' He traced his chin again with the heel of his thumb. 'No, I've been foolish but I see my opportunity now. I think it's time he saw them again, don't you? Something impressive to catch their attention. *That* will end their game.'

The Director tapped firmly on the desk. 'While the rest of the world watches our little show of smoke and mirrors and is thoroughly distracted, we'll let Friedman have his moment. Do this well and I think their search for truth will be over. Our work will be complete if we return Friedman to them.'

He stood up and for a moment considered his words. 'Miss Vernan,' he said softly, 'as a Level Five employee, I have opened your eyes to the world of Suppression. I've taken you to see dwellings underground where the work of our department can be seen in all its glory. But what you've seen at Down Street and the British

Museum stations is really just the tip of the iceberg.' This phrase made him laugh and his eyes widen. 'Since you're a future employee of Level Six of the Black Chamber I'd be willing to show you a whole world of secrets underground.' He walked across the room and slid his hand over the statue of a small horse, its front hooves raised in action. There was a clicking sound. A slow buzzing and then a picture frame on the wall swung clear of its fixing. Kerrith peered closely. Behind the picture frame was a series of shelves. The Director reached up on to the shelves and took down a small manila folder tied with red ribbon. He turned to face her.

'I think you're ready now to know about Site Three,' he said.

Kerrith felt a shiver run up her spine. 'Site Three, sir?'

'Site Three has had many code-names. Burlington, Hawthorn, even Subterfuge and Turnstile. Site Three's what we're calling it now.'

'It, sir?'

The Director passed over the folder. 'Site Three's an underground city, Kerrith. A hidden world far below ground.'

Kerrith untied the ribbon and turned to the front document. A whole booklet of facts about a town built below earth in case the country ever suffered a nuclear attack.

Kerrith looked up.

'Pretty incredible, don't you think?' he said. 'What we manage to keep from the British public.'

Kerrith swallowed hard. She flicked through the file to a yellowed map. 'Why are you showing me this?' she asked.

'Site Three's the centre of all we do here,' the Director clarified. 'Site Three gives us the capacity to really break our enemies on a major scale. Let's think about all those who over the last few months and years have begun to toy with the edges of MS 408. All those who've tried to find a voice for something which should never be spoken. We need to break them. So we cause a distraction.'

Kerrith was trying hard to keep up.

'A terrible disease, let's say. What could be more natural than that? It's perfect for clogging the airwaves and covering every news site in the country and beyond. And it's perfect for removal.'

'Removal, sir?'

'Amid all the chaos, it would be sensible to take those who are contaminated away. Those showing signs of weakness. Under the cover of a natural disaster, we can remove from the streets all those who might eventually turn sympathiser with the team at Station X. A natural disaster gives us the chance to "cleanse". We'll do that at Site Three. And I suggest, Miss Vernan, that you and I should take a trip there before too long.'

'And what will happen there?' Kerrith asked, her throat so dry the words nearly evaporated as they left her throat.

The Director lifted his hand from the statue of the horse and the picture on the wall clicked back into place. 'We'll ensure the isolation of the team,' he said, 'by taking from the streets anyone we feel might have the potential to join them. And after we've returned to them a broken player in their game, it will be the team itself who gives up the chase. So much more satisfying if the enemy surrenders and walks away.'

Kerrith tapped her fingernail against her knee. 'When will this all happen?'

'Very soon. The phoney war's over. We mean business now.' He laughed. 'That team of wannabes and has-beens have no idea what's about to begin.'

'What the peanut butter sandwich is that noise?' spluttered Hunter.

It was dark. Brodie banged her head against the window as she sat up and a procession of woolly pompoms hit her on the nose. She fumbled in her bag,

271

grabbed the mobile phone which was playing the theme tune of The Muppets and snapped it open.

It was difficult to hear Tandi's voice. She was speaking quickly. Her words jumbled. Brodie tried to make sense of what she heard. Then the line went blank.

'She hung up?' mumbled Hunter, his hair framing his face like a crumpled halo. 'She wakes us up in the middle of the night and she hangs up on us?'

Brodie rubbed her eyes. 'She said she's sending us a picture,' she cried.

'Oh, very nice,' said Hunter. 'Just what I need to help me get back to sleep. How very thoughtful of her. Very kind.'

Brodie didn't have time to answer him before the phone buzzed again and vibrated in her hand.

She looked down at the screen.

One new message.

She clicked 'open'.

A fuzzy scanned image came into focus.

It took a while to work out what she saw. What was listed as a picture was in fact a piece of text. It was an article from a newspaper. Brodie scrolled through the image and read the text aloud:

Artefacts from tragic *Titanic* are to go on sale

Next weekend, to mark the 97th anniversary of the sinking of the *Titanic* after it collided with an iceberg, there will be an auction of artefacts salvaged from the fateful maiden voyage.

Among the precious pieces is a photograph of Madeleine Astor which was taken on Christmas Day, in Paris, in 1911. The photograph is expected to raise at least £5,000 because of the controversy surrounding the couple.

Poor Madeleine, married to the world's richest man, John Jacob Astor IV, was to become a widow at the age of 18, only four months after the photograph was taken. She survived the sinking of the 'Ship of Dreams' but her husband was to perish along with 1,516 other passengers and crew.

The couple had been taking an extended honeymoon after their marriage in September 1911. They were occupying the 'millionaire's cabin' having decided to travel to Europe and Northern Africa to try and escape the gossip back home in New York that surrounded their marriage.

Mr Astor had divorced his wife Ava who was the mother of his two children. His eldest son, Vincent, was only a year younger than Madeleine when the new marriage took place. The couple planned to start a new family together and Madeleine was five months pregnant at the time the ship hit the iceberg.

Reports suggest that at first the Astors were not keen to board the lifeboats. Eventually, John Jacob Astor IV helped his wife on to one of the small vessels, obeying the 'woman and children first' rule, although many male passengers bribed their way on to life-rafts.

Mr Astor's body was eventually recovered on April 22nd and given the identification number '124'.

The following items were found on him: a gold watch, gold and diamond cufflinks, a diamond ring, £225 in notes, $2,240 in notes and various gold and silver pieces and coins. He was eventually buried at Trinity cemetery, New York.

On August 14th 1912 Mrs Astor gave birth to their son. She named him after her husband, registering him as John Jacob Astor V.

April 11th 2009

'All very nice,' said Hunter, rubbing his head. 'Moving, even. You've got to feel for her, and—'

'Knew Fabyan would make sense of it! It was the wrong John Jacob Astor!' Sheldon jabbered. Tusia peered again at the article as Sheldon ploughed on. 'He was wearing the ring. It says so in the article. "A diamond ring". And we thought John Jacob Astor died on the *Titanic*.'

'Well, he did,' said Kitty nervously.

'*One* of them did. But his wife was going to have a baby. Don't you see – that's someone who survived on the *Titanic* but wouldn't have been listed because he wasn't even born then! The baby was called John Jacob. *Technically he is a survivor* of the *Titanic. He* must have inherited his father's ring.' He paused. 'Life, not death's important here. We need to track down the John Jacob Astor who survived if we want to find out about that ring.'

Tusia was smiling broadly, her face illuminated by the glow of Sicknote's battery-operated torch.

'This is fabulous news,' said Hunter. 'No, seriously. It is. Tomorrow we can start thinking about the surviving Astor and the ring.' He looked again at Tusia. 'Seriously, Toots. You're freaking me out with all that grinning.'

Brodie had to admit her friend did look a little like

a Halloween pumpkin.

'Life not death,' said Tusia airily.

Hunter shot Brodie a knowing look.

'It's about life,' Tusia added again.

'Yes, it's all about life, Toots.'

Tusia's smile fractured into a glare.

'What I mean is, we've been focusing on death. And that led us to the pyramid tomb. But what we didn't think about was what Mad Jack Fuller got up to in his life.'

Brodie shot to her feet and banged her head sharply on the roof of the Matroyska. '*Paths of glory*,' she exclaimed, barely acknowledging the bump on her head.

'Oh, baked Alaska,' groaned Hunter. 'Now what've I missed?'

Brodie sat down again and rubbed her head. '*Paths of glory lead but to the grave*,' she said, 'and all we've done is make straight for the grave. I think Tusia's right and Mad Jack Fuller made quite a few paths of glory while he was alive and *that's* where we should be focusing. The pyramid grave is great because it shows we're on the right lines, but if we want to find out why Jack Fuller was important and how he can help us with MS 408, maybe we've got to look at what he did in his lifetime.' She scanned the camper van hopefully. 'Get me?'

Hunter looked round the others in the van. Oh, they got her all right. Seemed time for rest was over. They had work to do.

'Calm down, Brodie. You're not making any sense.'

Brodie held the mobile phone away from her head. Her granddad had a tendency to shout into the receiver and she feared for her eardrums.

Brodie rubbed her ear and tried again to explain their plan to her granddad. 'We're trying to find a tower that was important to Jack Fuller *when he was alive.*'

'A tower, you say?'

'Yes. Because of the link with the Tower of the Winds and the picture of the tower on the gravestone in the abbey.'

'The tower which was on fire, you mean?'

Brodie nodded and then remembered words were important if she was to make her granddad understand. 'Tandi and Fabyan said it's about time we all tried to get together. Tandi said there are things she's found out. Things she wants to share.' Brodie waited for her granddad to answer. 'Hello. Are you still there?'

When he spoke again, her grandfather's voice was a little husky. 'I know there's things she wants to show you,' he said. 'Things I've asked her to collect.'

Brodie couldn't follow what he was talking about. That didn't matter for the moment. There was a buzzing on the line. A crackle of interference. 'But, Brodie,' cut in her granddad in a voice which sounded distorted somehow, like it had been stretched. 'You have to be careful getting around.'

'Why?'

'They've just announced on the news there's a new epidemic of bird flu. They're taking people into quarantine. Students at universities, schools and colleges. They're banning public meetings and rallies. Trying to lessen the chance of contamination.'

Brodie pulled the phone closer to her ear.

'The news is full of it. Warning people not to meet in large groups. They're warning about huge numbers of deaths. Even comparing it to the Great Smog of 1952.'

Brodie had to check she was hearing properly. 'The Great Smog?'

Her granddad's voice down the end of the line explained. 'The air in London in 1952 was filled with pollution. Thousands of people died.'

Brodie had never heard of it.

'You just need to be careful, Brodie. Wherever Fuller's tower is, you have to be careful.'

'I will. I will. I promise.'

There was a moment of silence. His voice was so quiet suddenly, she had to press the phone hard against her ear. 'Just know whatever happens, I want the best for you.'

The Director rubbed his hands. He was having a particularly good morning. He was enjoying the distraction. The cleansing operation was going well. And more than that, he had a location. He wasn't sure why Jack Fuller's tower was so important to the team. That didn't matter. It was important to him now.

He passed the transcript of the phone conversation across the table. 'Find Fuller's tower, Miss Vernan. A friend of ours has a meeting to attend there.'

Tandi and Fabyan pushed open the door to Mr Bray's room at Bletchley Park Mansion. 'Do you know what we're looking for?'

'A biscuit tin,' said Tandi.

'You hungry then?'

Tandi didn't bother to answer. She went straight to the chest of drawers. Mr Bray had been precise and very clear in his instructions. The tin was exactly where he'd said it would be. And the envelope too, just as he promised, hidden at the bottom.

Tandi put the tin back and then handed what she'd

found to Fabyan. 'One more check in the Listening Post before we leave?' she said.

Fabyan nodded. In the light it was still possible to see the indentation of a key pressed firmly into the envelope before he folded it in half and pushed it in his pocket.

19

Quartet of Weird

'Where d'you get that?'

'Call me a genius if you like, B, but I can track down a good breakfast within a hundred-mile radius.'

Hunter was standing at the door of the Matroyska as the morning mist lifted behind him, his arms laden with bags. The smell of bacon butties and a mix of spice and orange peel filled the air.

'Not *that*,' said Brodie, helping him into the Matroyska and relieving him of half the bags he carried. '*That*,' she said, waving the end of a French stick at a piece of paper flapping beneath his chin.

'Oh yeah,' said Hunter, putting the other bags down in Sicknote's lap and pulling the sheet of paper from inside his jumper. 'This was a result too.'

Brodie grabbed the paper from him and tried in vain to shake out the creases before reading out the title printed in block letters across the top. 'FULLER'S FOLLIES . . . a map to the madness.'

'I got it from the church,' went on Hunter, breaking off the end of the French stick and munching on it.

'*You broke into the church*,' moaned Tusia, whose eyes were still bleary with sleep, but still capable, it seemed, of delivering their trademark glare of disapproval.

'No, for the love of banana smoothies, I didn't break into the church. It's Maundy Thursday. The church is open for some special foot-washing service.'

'Foot washing? Why on earth would the church be . . . ?'

Brodie held her hands up. 'If we could just focus on the map, please.'

There was a mumble of apology as Smithies began to hand out the breakfast.

'This is totally, absolutely, brilliant.'

'Knew you'd like it, B,' winked Hunter.

'It seems Mad Jack really was into building things,' said Brodie, after she'd taken the sandwich offered to her and propped the map up against the steamy window of the Matroyska so everyone could see. 'And according to this, he actually did build a tower, right near here.

FULLER'S FOLLIES ... A MAP TO THE MADNESS

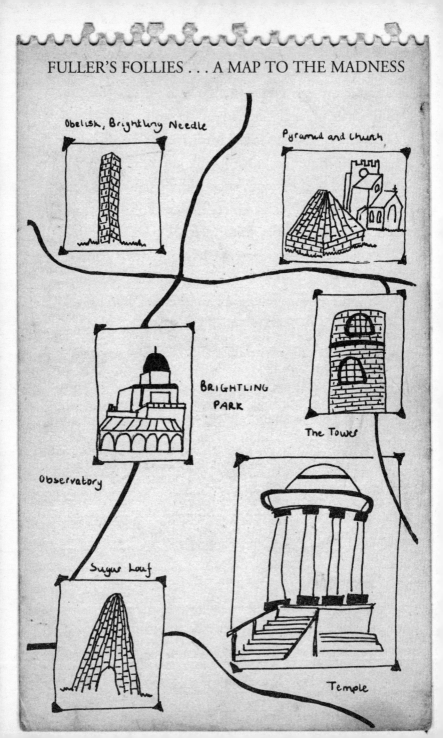

Obelisk, Brightling Needle

Pyramid and Church

Observatory

BRIGHTLING PARK

The Tower

Sugar Loaf

Temple

The map says he built three other things too. That makes a quartet of weirdness.' She smiled. 'A needle, a temple and something called the Sugar Loaf.'

'So I did a good job then, getting us a map,' grinned Hunter.

'You really did. I can't imagine this is going to take us any time at all,' she said. 'Any clues left behind have to be at the tower.' She took a bite from her sandwich. 'I've got a really good feeling about this.'

The door swung open wide. Friedman staggered backwards and stumbled to the ground.

'You better get up from there,' the nurse sniffed. The revulsion she felt was not even faintly disguised.

'I need to— There's someone I—'

The nurse raised her hands to silence him. 'No time for that now,' she glared. 'You have a visitor.'

For the tiniest of moments Friedman allowed his heart to feel hope.

'No. No. No. This isn't good!' Tandi was sitting by the computer screen.

'What?' yelped Fabyan. 'You lost connection?'

'Worse!' shrieked Tandi. 'Much worse! Look!'

The cursor was moving erratically across the screen.

'It's being controlled remotely! Someone must have

worked out we've linked into the system. The cursor's being moved by someone back at the Chamber!'

Fabyan stared at the screen.

The cursor began to travel fluidly. It snapped to the bottom of the page and clicked on an icon. The screen flashed white. A blank document opened. The cursor flashed. Then it moved slowly across the screen leaving a trail of text in its wake. The first line was in capital letters set across the centre of the page:

WE HAVE A MESSAGE FOR YOU!

Mad Jack Fuller's tower was almost hidden by trees. It was about a quarter of a mile south-east of Brightling Park and Hunter calculated it was about ten metres high.

Brodie was so excited. She couldn't help but imagine the Lady of Shalott locked in a tower just like it and forced to look down as the world passed her by. 'Why did Fuller build it?' she asked as they cut their way through the trees. 'Surely not to keep people prisoner?'

Hunter looked down at the map and the notes printed on the reverse. 'No one's really sure. There's a theory that the tower was put up so Mad Jack could keep an eye on workmen who were building other things. But the dates don't really fit.'

Brodie looked up through the shadow cast by the

thick stone walls. 'Can we get inside?' she asked, striding towards a gated doorway. A push against the metal bars and the swing of the gate gave the answer.

Inside, the tower stretched up towards the sky and an iron staircase curled around the internal wall. A metal walkway stretched across the tower, breaking the view of the sky above into tiny squares. Hunter read more from the notes. 'There were wooden floors,' he said, 'but according to this, some local boys set fire to them.'

'Shall we climb up?' said Tusia, making for the metal stairwell.

'Oh no,' groaned Sicknote, who'd only just made his way into the tower. 'I cannot be party to any more climbing.'

Tusia was undeterred. She clambered on to the metal stairwell and pushed her way up to the opening in the roof. 'The view's amazing,' she called down. 'Come and see.'

Brodie gripped tightly to the handrail and climbed behind her friend. 'Will it take my weight?' she called nervously.

'Not after that extra hot cross bun,' yelled up Hunter.

Brodie's hand tightened on the rail.

The view from the top was beautiful. The village of Brightling stretching out in front of them framed like a picture, or a reflection in a mirror.

But the reflection told them nothing.

Nothing at all.

They took it in turns then, to climb to the top and look out. They worked in pairs to skirt round the tower, running their hands along the brickwork, scratching at the lichen lining of the moss. They looked for clues. Anything at all which could have been a message left as a voice from the past.

It was Smithies who broke the silence. 'I think we have to face the fact there's nothing here,' he said quietly. 'Whatever message Mad Jack Fuller left behind for us to find isn't hidden in his tower.'

Tusia took the map from Hunter's hand. 'Maybe the message is in something else he built *with* a tower,' she suggested. 'Don't forget there was a "quartet of weird". Fuller built other buildings here. Maybe we should look at them too.' And with that she led the way out of the tower and off through the trees and back towards the road.

It was as she cleared the protection of the trees that Brodie's mobile phone began to ring.

'I can't hear you, Tandi!' Brodie cradled the phone tight to her ear. 'You need to slow down. You're making no sense.'

The line was breaking up. And the words Miss

Tandari used tumbled from her mouth in a chaotic jumble. Brodie tried to make sense of what she heard. And then, when the truth settled in her mind, she began to shake.

'You're absolutely sure?'

There was only one word offered in answer.

'And you think it's to do with Friedman?'

Again a single word in response.

Brodie shut her eyes. 'And you've told my granddad?'

The line fizzed and crackled. Brodie heard only the final sentence: 'You need to be careful and you need to be quick!'

Then the line went dead.

The rest of the team gathered round as Brodie tried to explain what had happened. 'It's not good! Level Five are on to us again. Somehow they know we've made a connection to Jack Fuller,' she said, replaying the frantic conversation she'd just had. 'Tandi says Level Five want us to find the message at Fuller's tower.'

'They *want* us to find it? I thought they wanted us to leave MS 408 alone. I thought all this was because they didn't want us to find the truth!' Hunter was angry.

'I know! But now things have changed!'

'But we couldn't find anything at the tower,' said

Sheldon. 'There was no message!'

'So it must be at a tower built on to one of the other things Fuller built,' said Tusia.

'OK. So we keep looking,' said Smithies. 'We work through Fuller's quartet.'

Brodie could barely speak. 'It's seven o'clock.'

Hunter looked confused.

'Tandi says they want us to find Fuller's message before midnight,' Brodie explained. 'We've got five hours.'

'And then what?'

'If we don't find the message by then, someone's going to die.'

The Brightling Needle stretched about twenty metres into the air, on top of a hill known as Brightling Beacon.

'The second one in the quartet,' panted Tusia as they circled around its base. 'It's sort of a tower.'

Brodie wasn't sure. 'Why was this here?' she asked, her voice catching in her throat.

Hunter peered through the fading light at the notes on the map. 'No idea. Just something he built.'

'And something he didn't bother to put any writing or inscriptions on,' moaned Sheldon from his position on his knees at the base of the needle.

'It's just an obelisk,' said Sicknote, joining Sheldon

as he scrabbled at the base searching for any signs or plaques.

Sheldon looked at him quizzically.

'Just a tall thing stuck in a field.'

Brodie ran her fingers through her hair. 'But it makes no sense. Why would he build it? Where's the message? What does it mean?'

'It means nothing,' said Kitty. 'It can't do, can it? It's just here.'

Brodie's heart was banging out the seconds in her head. How could this have become so hard?

'What's the time?'

'Nearly eight.' Hunter couldn't look at her.

'What's building number three?' gasped Tusia, reaching for the map. 'What about this temple he built? Could that have a tower? Should we go there next?'

Brodie grabbed the map as they ran back down the hill to the waiting Matroyska. It seemed the best way to answer.

'Why would any sane man build a temple in the middle of the English countryside?' asked Sheldon as the van bumped along the narrow lane, Kitty's motorbike following in its wake.

'He wasn't sane,' cut in Hunter.

'But why a temple?'

'I don't know,' said Hunter, searching the map again for clues. 'But the message has got to be there! The next building on the list.'

They pulled the van over to the side of the road and peered across the valley.

'There. D'you see?' Tusia was pointing out of the window through the beam of the headlights. 'It looks like a Greek temple. The sort of thing the Dilettanti Society would have loved. Come on!'

'But there's no tower,' groaned Brodie.

'We have to check!' said Hunter. 'Supposing the message is here. Supposing we miss it! They say someone'll die!'

Brodie looked down at one of her watches. It was nearly nine. They'd got three hours. Two more of Fuller's crazy buildings to search. But if they didn't go to the temple, there was a chance the very clue they needed would be missed.

'We split up,' Brodie said.

Hunter shook his head. 'One hundred and seventy-nine minutes, B! We can't!'

'It's the only way.'

'Wasn't it splitting up and letting Tandi and Fabyan go off on their own that led to Level Five knowing what we're up to?' Hunter blurted.

'But if I go with Kitty on her bike and check out this

place called the Sugar Loaf,' Brodie said, jabbing at the map, 'and you check the temple, then we'll save time. We've got to hurry!'

'What on earth's a Sugar Loaf?' called Kitty as she hurried behind Brodie down a thin and overgrown track beside the road where she'd abandoned her motorbike.

Brodie tried to talk as she ran, her voice leaking out in spluttered gulps. 'It's a pointed building that looks like a Victorian cone of sugar,' she said. 'At least we know why Fuller built this one.'

'We do?' came Kitty's voice from behind her.

Brodie swallowed and tried to read from the map with a torch as she hurried onwards. 'It says Fuller once made a bet he could see the spire of St Giles church in Dallington from his home in Brightling Park. When he got home and found he couldn't, he had builders work overnight to put up this thing that looks like a church spire so he'd win the bet. Look, see. There's a picture of St Giles' church spire. And here,' she said, pushing her way through the overhanging branches, 'is Mad Jack Fuller's Sugar Loaf.'

'But where's the message in that?' said Kitty.

'Seeing things that aren't there?' said Brodie. 'Being deceived?' It all fitted with what they knew, but Brodie had no idea how it helped them now. She bent down with her hands on her knees to catch her breath. 'It's a kind of tower, isn't it?' she panted. 'It's the last building. This has to be the place.'

Brodie circled the base of the structure and her heart quickened as the torchlight flashed on a sign. At last. Some information. Some clues they could use! Maybe this was the message!

But the sign told them little more than they already knew.

'People lived in here?' said Kitty. 'How could they have? It's tiny.'

Brodie stepped through the doorway. It was small, the ceiling spiralling upwards to the sky.

She walked to the window and shone the torch out across the fields falling away into the distance. 'I don't understand,' she said at last. 'It's the last building in the quartet. What are we supposed to find?' She pressed the heels of her palms against her eyes and the world went black. 'If we're supposed to follow Jack Fuller's paths of glory then where on earth do they lead?'

Kitty put her arm round Brodie's shoulder. Her voice, when she spoke, was little more than a whisper. 'You know I've learnt loads from you lot,' she said. 'Loads and loads, about stories and pictures and music and signs. And at first it was hard for me to think like you did, to see the things you noticed or to hear the things you heard.' She glanced around erratically, obviously scared to make a suggestion.

Brodie took her hands down from her face. Her vision swirled with dots and flecks.

'There's one more place,' said Kitty softly. 'It's not one of the four follies. Not something he built just for fun.' She paused, and took the crumpled map they'd used and turned it over. 'See. Somewhere very serious. Fuller built it for study. Because he wanted to find out all he could about how the universe worked. We've still got two hours. Jack Fuller's observatory's the only place left to try.'

'There's nothing at the temple,' said Hunter, his face wet with sweat.

'Knew there wouldn't be,' said Brodie.

'You did?'

'Well, Kitty did really. She worked it out.'

'Worked what out?'

Brodie tried to explain. 'The four follies are great but they can't really be where the answers are. All our searching in the past has been connected to people's work. Important work, like poems and pictures.'

'You think building some Greek temple in the middle of a field wasn't work?' said Hunter.

'It was just symbolic,' said Brodie. 'It didn't do anything. Didn't mean anything.' The inscription on Fuller's pyramid said that *paths of glory lead but to the grave*. And we haven't been looking at paths of glory. Things that really meant something.' She shook out the tattered map in her hand. 'We've been looking at things he made just for fun. But Fuller built an observatory to look at the stars. Now, that's got to be a tower with purpose, don't you think?' She glanced at her Greenwich Mean Time watch. 'Quarter past ten! It has to be there.'

'I have a question,' said Hunter.

Brodie felt her shoulders tighten.

'What the Jaffa Cake are we waiting for?'

The Director looked up from the map. A location had been circled in red. 'You've done well again, Miss Vernan.'

Kerrith's lips twitched into a smile. She still enjoyed his praise even though she didn't need him to tell her she'd been brilliant. It seemed the team's obsession with dead people was going to pay off after all. Fuller's tower was perfect. And now she had everything she needed.

A Tower of Light

'This can't be right,' whispered Brodie, hunched over and ducking her head behind an overgrown hedge.

'It's what it says on the map,' said Smithies.

'But how can we find any clues in there?' she said.

'And how d'we get past them?' said Sheldon, gesturing towards two huge guard dogs that were making long, low growling noises and baring their teeth through the bars of a metal gate which blocked the pathway.

'It's a private home,' hissed Hunter. 'They couldn't make it any clearer.'

'This can't be right,' Brodie said. 'Paths of glory and all that. It *has* to be here.'

Tusia grabbed Brodie's shoulder in an obvious

attempt to encourage her, but Brodie shook her hand away. 'We can't be wrong. We've got one and a half hours! You didn't hear Tandi. She was so scared. Someone will die if we don't get to the right place on time!'

Hunter hid his face in his hands as if trying to shut out any distractions.

'Fuller's tower!' said Brodie. 'A place of work. Somewhere to look for answers. The observatory's perfect. It fits!'

She strode towards the gate and the dogs on the other side barred their teeth once more and began to growl again.

'Paths of glory. Lead to the grave. Leading. Glory. It's got to be here!'

Sicknote stood up beside her and tried, as Tusia had done, to reassure her by patting her shoulder.

Brodie looked up into the sky. A mist was drawing in. They'd found nothing. And it was nearly quarter to eleven. She reached for the paper and blazed the torch on the map. What had they missed?

And then, it was like a light flashed in her head. A search beam cutting through the gloom. A jolt of memory. The day before this whole adventure really began. She'd stood on a bridge across a river, under a light burning brightly in the middle of the day. The light had been the answer. She'd searched and she'd waited, but inside the base of the lamppost on the bridge spanning the river, she'd found what she was looking for. Answers about Operation Veritas and all she'd been called to do. The memory washed across her like a wave in the sea. Then another. A part of Fuller's story they'd chosen, until now, to ignore.

'We're in the wrong place!' she yelled, and her voice caused even the dogs to silence. She looked down at her watches. 'We'll be too late!'

Hunter grabbed her by the wrists. 'B, come on, calmly, tell us.'

'Light,' she blurted. 'Paths of glory means light. It *always* meant light. Shakespeare's statue in London was all about darkness being ignorance. We're miles away from where we should be.'

'So where *should* we be?' Hunter pressed, not loosening the hold on her arms.

'Beachy Head Belle Toute Lighthouse! Tusia told us about it when we first found out about Fuller, but we got so caught up with his follies we forgot.' She drew breath. 'The lighthouse. The *tower of light*.'

'Brodie. Explain.' Smithies' voice was firm and deliberate.

'I remember!' Tusia cut in. 'Fuller ordered the building of a lighthouse on the cliffs of Beachy Head. A tower looking out to sea. To other places. That could link to America. Maybe even to Avalon. That might be why we found the funeral medal with the Declaration of Independence.'

'A tower of light like the tower on the grave in Westminster Abbey!' Sheldon added. 'So that's where we've got to go!'

'I'll take you,' Kitty said suddenly. 'The motorbike. It'll be quicker than the Matroyska. We've got just over an hour! Come on!'

Kerrith drummed her polished fingernails on the manila folder in her lap. She was trying not to focus on the passenger beside her. She was thinking about what would happen if her plan was successful.

Even in her wildest dreams she couldn't have hoped for such rapid promotion, or to have been trusted with such an important secret. The details she'd read about Site Three and its underground world still buzzed through her brain.

The Director had been very clear. She had one thing left to do. And it was all about appearance.

She was to return the traitor Friedman to them. And she was particularly pleased with how well she'd managed to dovetail her plans with those from Station X. She enjoyed the appearance of the plan.

Appearance, after all, was absolutely everything.

* * *

It was dark.

They drove through villages and hamlets and then along the coast until the cliffs pulled up as great white peaks along the shore. The earth severed from the sea, gashes in the ground, scarred white with chalk.

'It's like the end of the world,' said Kitty as she pulled the bike to a stop.

Brodie couldn't answer.

By the time they reached the lighthouse, a thick mist was swirling in from the sea. The sky was starless and there was no moon. Kitty kept the headlight of the bike glowing.

Brodie swung down from the bike and took off her leather gloves. This was it then. Jack Fuller's tower of light. They'd been distracted by the sights and follies of Brightling. But this was his *work*. The building put up in a place where he knew it would save lives.

She took off her helmet and steadied herself against the gate which marked the end of the small and rutted road leading up to the lighthouse.

It was five to midnight.

In the road stood a woman masked in shadow.

The sound of clapping broke the air. Slow and rhythmic clapping.

Brodie felt her stomach contract.

'Brodie?' Kitty was stepping closer. 'Is she the woman from Westminster Abbey?'

Kerrith began to laugh.

'She's here to stop us,' Brodie said.

Kerrith moved forward into the beam cast by the headlight. 'That's a little unfair. It wasn't always my mission,' she said. 'For a while, it's true, we wanted you to stop your research into MS 408 but it soon became clear to us that letting you continue with your little exploits would eventually be to our advantage.' She flicked at a moth circling in the light. 'But you went too far when you began to involve the public. Search for knowledge is like an epidemic. It must be cut off at the source when it begins to affect others.' The moth hit the headlight and burned. 'Do you know what the time is, Brodie? I know you're keen never to lose track.'

Brodie looked down at her Greenwich Mean Time watch. One minute to twelve. The midnight deadline seconds away.

'It's about time we had a little light on the situation.' Kerrith raised her hands in the air and, controlled somehow by this movement, the lamp from the lighthouse on the hill flickered into life, silhouetting the forms of two men as they ran away.

Brodie squinted as the lamp blazed and then began

to turn, sweeping great shafts of clarity across the cliffs and the ocean, joining the worlds of sea and the shore in pulsing cascades of light. For the first time, Brodie could see the lighthouse clearly. Strangely ugly and square it stood like a beacon at the end of the path. And the lamp rotated. Seen then unseen. Darkness then light.

'I expect you've been wondering why Friedman never returned to your team. I know you've heard his side of the story now but it can't have stopped you wondering why he could never explain things to you face to face.'

Brodie felt anger swelling inside her.

'The answer's in the light.'

Brodie looked up the path and peered into the circling splashes of radiance. What did Kerrith mean? How could the answer be in the light?

And then she saw it. A man spread against the glass.

She knew at once it was Friedman.

She lurched forward and Kitty grabbed at her. 'Brodie, wait—'

Kerrith laughed again. 'You wanted to find a message. Well, this is it. If you're left long enough believing no one's listened to your side of the story, then life no longer seems worth living. If you're doubted and all men call you a liar, then life's nothing but pain.

That's the message, Brodie. That's Friedman's message to you.'

Brodie struggled to break free of Kitty's grasp.

Kerrith held up her hand. 'You see, we were naive at first. We thought simply telling you Friedman was involved in your mother's death would be enough. We forgot we were dealing with people obsessed with truth. And once you knew what really happened with your mother, we realised you'd no longer hate him. But what would happen if we kept the truth from Friedman? Never released him? Never told him you kept ringing? Kept him in the dark?' She waved towards the lamp of the lighthouse. 'There's your answer, Brodie.'

Brodie fought again against Kitty's hold. 'What have you told him?'

'Nothing!' hissed Kerrith. 'That's the real genius of the plan. All this time, when he hoped you'd be searching for him, we've told him absolutely nothing.'

She began to walk away and then she turned one more time. 'Let me make it totally clear for you. We control events, disasters and truth. You've all taken on a battle that's far too big for you. We'll always be in control.'

Brodie broke free of Kitty's hold. She pushed her way up the hill towards the lighthouse, the chalky path slipping and skittering below her feet.

'Brodie. Wait!'

Brodie didn't listen. Kitty couldn't hold her back with her hands or her words. But it was suddenly clear it wasn't Kitty who was calling.

A car skidded to a halt beside her. The doors flung open and Tandi and Fabyan hurried out. 'Brodie, wait!'

'It's Friedman!' Brodie gasped. 'He's up on the tower.'

'Brodie, listen first.' Tandi's eyes were wild, her hair swept behind her like a sail on a boat.

Brodie looked down the hill as Kerrith strode off towards the main road. Then she looked up towards the lighthouse where the lamp still flashed and turned, silhouetting a figure against the glass. 'There isn't time!'

'We must make time.' Another voice. Brodie turned to see her granddad was clambering from the car. 'I always meant to tell you, Brodie. I thought if I waited till you were older, you'd understand.'

'Understand what?'

The old man leant on his stick. Tandi put her arm round his shoulder. He took a piece of paper from his pocket. Above their heads a seagull circled and shrieked. 'Before you speak to Friedman . . .' She saw tears glint in his eyes.

The seagull circled again and called out once more, low and loud and mournful.

'This is a letter to Friedman from your mother. She left it with me, to give to him if anything happened to her. I never did.'

The seagull circled again. 'Granddad! We have to hurry!'

Something in his face stopped her.

'It's something your mother never had the chance to tell him.' He took her hand. 'The letter says Friedman is your father, Brodie.'

Brodie ran.

The sea spray beat against her. The light sliced through the mist. And her heart pounded in her chest so she could barely breathe.

Friedman was her father!

She stumbled as she ran, hearing Tandi and Fabyan calling to her.

A metal gate barred the way. She pushed it open. An unmade wall lined the footing of the tower. She scrambled up it. Then she burst through the door to the tower and inside.

The wind circled in the stairwell and her own steps echoed as she climbed. Then she pushed open the door to the lantern room, into the blinding light.

She struggled past the mirrors and lenses lining the walls as the light spun and the beam was channelled so it filled the room. Then she stood still. She could see him. He was outside on the walkway that ringed the lantern room.

He had his back to the light. Was facing out to the sea. And his hands were outstretched like a cross, hanging on to the railings. Then she saw his hands were tied, his arms looped over the rails so he hung the other side of the walkway above the water.

She struggled to understand. They'd left him here to die! Was he dead already? Was she too late?

She stepped out on to the walkway, moving first in light and then in dark; patches of shadow and then of brilliance.

Through the roar of the sea surging against the cliffs, she yelled, 'Friedman. It's me.'

'Brodie?' His voice was jagged, as if it had been, for months, unused.

Closer now, she could see his clothes were tattered, his frame shrunken, his hair matted. And the ropes that bound him dug into his skin. His feet were pushed hard against the wall in a desperate attempt to take his weight, yet they scratched and slipped as she watched, the ropes cutting tighter into his wrists.

'What do I do?' She reached forward and grabbed for his hand.

'I loved your mother with all my heart, Brodie.'

'Hold on! There'll be people coming!' she urged.

But she knew more certainly than she'd known anything before, time was running out. The weight of his body was pulling down on his arms. His chest couldn't draw in air. If she didn't get him free of the ropes, he'd suffocate.

She'd solved puzzles and cryptograms and conundrums and enigmas. But centimetres away, Friedman hung dying and she didn't know how to save him.

'Hold on, please, please hold on!' she yelled, lurching to her feet and staggering along the walkway.

She crashed into the lantern room and ran her hand along the walls. The lantern rotated round and round, the sealed beam sweeping across her. She had to make the light permanent, so she could see what to do. She scratched at the floor and eased one of the rotting planks free. She picked it up and jammed it hard against the lantern and the wall. The end grated on the lenses and mirrors that lined the walls. There was a creaking noise like a giant tearing sound. Then a shudder and a long, low groan.

And the lantern stopped moving.

The light burned bright and unbroken in one continuous beam.

Brodie fumbled to her feet and hurried once more,

circling the lamp. She had to find something to cut Friedman free. But there was nothing.

She bent down and yanked another wooden strut from the floor. Then she swung it hard against the wall of mirrors. The glass shattered, and Brodie covered her head against the fragments raining down on her. Then she selected a shard of glass and raced back outside to where Friedman hung above the sea.

His eyes were closed.

'Please,' she begged. 'Hold on!'

The light burned her. The brilliance of a million candles blazing like the midday sun on her skin.

She lay on her stomach. 'I'm going to cut the ropes,' she said. 'Get you free.'

But the shard of glass slipped. She dragged it against the hessian binding but it wouldn't cut the rope.

Friedman stirred. 'It's not worth it, Brodie,' he whispered. 'No point, you see . . .'

'No!' she yelled, frantic again. She swallowed a cry. 'You can't leave me. Granddad says you're my dad.'

Friedman opened his eyes.

In that moment, in those seconds when Brodie held the broken glass directly in the light of the lamp, there'd been a spark. A flicker of flame, made by the light and the shattered mirror combined. Tongues of fire burned at the rope around Friedman's left arm. He cried out as the fire licked at his skin. The rope fell away, so he was suspended now just by the rope tied to his right wrist. He twisted his body round and stretched for the railing with his injured left hand. He couldn't reach. He was facing Brodie now. One arm still tied to the railings; the other burned and bleeding.

'Brodie!'

She reached forward. The rope on his right wrist was not strong enough to take all his weight. The fibres began to buckle and lift, the rope thinning.

He strained for the railings again, heaving his body upwards, and grabbed at the rail. The remaining rope burst free.

He was hanging now, with one hand round the railings.

Brodie clutched for his free hand.

'Brodie!'

His fingers were slipping. He wasn't strong enough to hold on.

Her arms locked.

She couldn't reach his other hand.

'Dad!'

His hand slipped.

He fell.

The Fallen Ones

The Director pressed his palms together. His pulse quickened.

The scroll lay unopened on his desk. The black ribbon like ink across the wood.

Slowly he slid the scroll free and pressed it flat.

He focused on each emblem in the corner and then the monogrammed letter 'T' before he allowed himself to read the words. It had been worth the wait.

'You have done well.'

There was a moment when Friedman hung there. Frozen in time, outstretched on the air as if it carried him. Then he plummeted away from her.

Below, the sound of an engine throbbed and whined.

An explosion. A plume of smoke and fire. A distant rumble and then a clattering as rocks and debris tumbled from the cliff top and crashed into the sea.

Brodie dropped her face against the cold concrete of the walkway.

The light blazed behind her. But it was still night.

It began to rain.

She heard a movement near her. She looked up.

Tandi knelt beside her, her clothes clinging to her in the rain, her words reaching Brodie through a muffled fog. 'It's OK.'

But it wasn't OK.

Tandi took Brodie's hand. She led her down through the lantern room, across the broken glass and down the twisted staircase to outside.

Brodie took in several things at once. The earth was scorched with fire. A single track burned towards the edge of the cliff. A thin expanse of cliff edge butted against the base of the building, which then fell away towards the sea.

Huddled in the space between the lighthouse and the edge of the cliff were three human forms framed by the light.

Kitty and Granddad and Fabyan. And on the ground between them, lying unmoving, was Friedman.

'Is he . . . ?' She couldn't say the word.

'I don't know, Brodie. We could see what was going to happen so Kitty rode her bike to try and break his fall. It cost her the bike – it went over the edge of the cliff. And I ran up to—'

'Is he dead?'

'I don't . . .'

Brodie ran towards the cliff edge. She threw herself down beside the stooped figures. The grass was wet, the rain still pelting against her shoulders. But she didn't feel it.

'Dad?'

Friedman opened his eyes.

Three days later, Brodie sat beside the fire in the sitting room of the Birling Gap Hotel. She tucked her feet under a blanket and stared across at the window. It was still raining. The sky had remained dark and misty grey, the clouds hiding a weakened sun. But the sound of the rain on the windows was strangely comforting. The wind rattled the wooden frames and Brodie shut her eyes and listened to the rain and the sea pounding at the shore. And she felt a contentment she didn't think she'd ever felt before.

The last few days were a fuzzy haze.

She'd sat with Friedman until the ambulance came.

It had churned its way up the cliff to the arc of light. The medics bandaged his bleeding hands and tended to Kitty's ribs, cracked when she'd broken Friedman's fall. There was little discussion from them about what had happened. It was a miracle they'd survived, they said, and that was all.

Friedman was kept in hospital overnight. His left hand was badly damaged and burned and the doctors feared he'd never fully recover the use of it. He seemed not to hear that. What he did hear, over and over again, was Brodie and Granddad explaining about the letter and the report they'd read about the day of her mother's accident.

Then he'd slept.

The hotel at Birling Gap was very accommodating. The manager was prepared to risk having unscreened guests despite the huge quarantine programme by the government trying to keep the bird flu epidemic under control.

By the time Brodie and her granddad returned from the hospital, the rest of the team were settled in. When Friedman was discharged he was given a room overlooking the sea. But he was too exhausted to look out of the window.

The rest sat now, listening to the rain and the ocean, trying to make sense of everything.

'A tower on fire, just like the gravestone showed us,' said Sheldon. 'A lighthouse. We should have known.'

Brodie nodded and tightened the folds of her blanket.

'And when you saved Friedman, B, it was mirrors and lights that did the job,' said Hunter. 'Every step of the way it's been about mirrors and light.'

'I thought he'd died though,' she said.

'Yeah, well. Phoenix from the flame, that Friedman,' said Hunter. 'You counted him out and he rose again.'

Brodie let the words wash over her. He'd risen again. Just like a firebird.

'And Kerrith missed it all,' said Smithies, his glasses pressed up high on to his forehead proving he was concentrating hard.

'Every last detail,' added Kitty, running her hand reassuringly across her side and wincing slightly. 'We saw her walk away and get into a car where the two men were waiting for her and then they drove off.'

'So she probably believes Friedman died?' mused Sicknote.

'I'm totally sure she won't believe a kid could have saved him!' said Hunter.

Smithies smiled. 'No doubt she thought he was so broken, so damaged, it didn't really matter. I bet she

313

doesn't believe there's a way back once you've slipped over the edge into despair.'

'And is there always a way back?' Sicknote asked.

'Maybe with time and the help of family, there is.' Smithies lowered his glasses to his eyes and Brodie was sure it was to cover the tears which sparkled there. 'I've been thinking,' he said. 'I need to tell Mrs Smithies what we're up to. I need to let her in on the secret of our quest.'

'You sure that's a good idea?'

'No. I'm not sure at all. But watching you and your granddad and Friedman. It just made me think we can try and protect people by hiding the truth from them. But sometimes, the truth's what they most need.' Brodie glanced around the room and smiled nervously at her granddad. She wasn't sure yet how she felt about him keeping the truth about Friedman from her. But she knew why he'd done it. 'When we get back to Bletchley, I'll tell her,' said Smithies, and there was only a tiny note of a tremor in his voice.

'We'll go back to Bletchley, then?' asked Kitty.

Smithies looked surprised. 'For a while at least.'

'And then?' asked Hunter.

'Back to MS 408?' suggested Tusia.

'Well, once we've checked the zebras have been well cared for by Gordon in our absence, we'll have to make

314

travel plans,' said Smithies. 'We can't begin to find out about what happened to Lady Astor's ring unless we track down the Astor family in the United States. And we have to find out what Thomas Jefferson Beale has to say about MS 408. I think Fuller's tower of light is telling us we've got to start looking across the sea if we want to find answers.'

'D'you really think if we look hard enough, we'll find a map to Avalon?' asked Tusia.

'I guess we'll have to keep digging to find out.'

'So America then?' said Brodie quietly.

Fabyan shuffled forward on his chair. 'I always knew we should be making more of the British-American links,' he grinned. 'I mean, after all, the first Study Group was an American-English affair, and the second group at Bletchley was made up of members from both sides of the pond. We should certainly think about some of the work done at Riverbank in the US. After all, the clue was in the architecture.'

It was obvious no one had any idea what he was talking about.

'Towers,' he said loudly. 'Towers of the Wind. It was all part of the Riverbank idea.'

'No. You've completely lost us,' said Tandi with a laugh.

Fabyan took a folded picture from his wallet, his

fingers hesitating for a second over a wedding photograph which he slipped back out of sight. 'Riverbank Lab,' he said triumphantly. 'Where William and Elizebeth Friedman first looked at the Voynich Manuscript. Look.' He passed the picture over. 'One of their proudest possessions at Riverbank was a windmill. A Tower of the Winds. See?'

Brodie stared at the picture. Her mind trickled over what Fabyan had said. William and Elizebeth Friedman. Workers at Riverbank Lab. Elizebeth. Such an odd spelling of the name. An 'e' in the centre instead of an 'a'. And yet. She closed her eyes. Brodie. Brodie Elizebeth Bray. The spelling of her middle name. Just the same. She should have known all along. The truth was there. Hidden. Elizebeth. Alex Bray had named her only daughter after Friedman's grandmother. Brodie's great-grandmother. Alex had included her father's family name for anyone who'd taken care to look.

Kitty was talking. About truth and decisions. Brodie shivered. It never ceased to amaze her how easily Kitty was able to express what everyone else had been thinking and was perhaps too scared to say. 'I mean, we've ended up with a whole lot of discoveries we've got to deal with now. This quest for answers doesn't half mix things up, doesn't it?' Kitty said.

'It certainly does,' said Smithies quietly.

'And the search for truth's tricky,' Kitty added, rubbing once more at her side.

'Difficult but not impossible,' said Granddad.

'But d'you think we'll ever get to Avalon?' Hunter said. 'I mean, really get there and find out what the words of MS 408 actually mean?'

Brodie remembered back to their morning in London and the statue of Shakespeare warning that darkness only came with ignorance. And she remembered the spark of fire produced by the lamp in the lighthouse. However fiercely it burned, the truth had to be worth pursuing. She believed that now, more deeply than ever.

Kitty smiled weakly. 'But what about the warning from Kerrith about giving up?' She clutched again at her injured side. 'Are we really up to the challenge?'

Brodie looked fondly across at the friend who'd claimed to have no special skills and yet had risked so much to save a man she didn't even know. She thought back to the conversation they'd once had about the things which drove them. Kitty had said Brodie was driven by a need for a happy ending. Maybe she was right. But in the moments beside the lighthouse, Brodie had seen the things which drove Kitty onward. A need to belong and take risks, whatever the cost. Maybe a happy ending only came if you took the ultimate risk. 'We're up to the challenge,' Brodie said. 'Whatever the risk, we're in too deep now.'

Epilogue

Brodie waited just for a moment before knocking.

The voice when it answered was tired but not weak. 'Come in.'

Brodie pushed open the door. Friedman's bed was facing the window. He was propped up on a raft of pillows, his bandaged hand visible above the sheets. At the sight of her, a light sparkled in his eyes.

Brodie pulled out the chair at the end of the bed and sat down.

He said nothing. He was waiting for her.

'Did you know,' she said at last, 'that you're my dad?'

Friedman shook his head. 'I hoped,' he said. 'But . . .' His eyes flickered but he didn't look away. 'Things with your mother were complicated, Brodie. I was a hard man to love. I was obsessed. Totally obsessed with MS 408.'

'We've found loads of people throughout history who were obsessed with it,' she said. 'A whole group called the Knights of Neustria.'

Friedman's face wrinkled into a frown. 'Seems to me there's lots I'll have to catch up on. But the thing is . . . obsession comes at a price, Brodie. Always.'

'How d'you mean?'

'We had a wonderful, beautiful summer, your mother and I. We thought we would change the world. We thought we'd discover secrets hidden for centuries. There was so much we were going to do. And then . . .'

'Then Mum got pregnant?'

He dropped his eyes. 'She didn't tell me, Brodie. I'd gone abroad to do more research. I was going to return and then things got complicated and . . .'

'And so you left her to have me alone?'

'It wasn't like that. I didn't know, and when I came back over a year later she'd had you and things had changed and . . . I became . . . ill . . .'

'Didn't you ever ask her?'

'Your mother had one child to look after. She didn't need another.'

'But you were with her when she died.'

'Yes. A couple of years after you were born, I was sure I'd found answers in Belgium. Your mum agreed to come with me. One last time. One last try.' His face flushed. 'Your grandfather looked after you. It was just a few days and while we were there . . .' His voice faltered. 'I realise now perhaps she was going to tell me. That I'd got well enough for her to explain. The night before she died she told me about the key. The one that worked the music box, remember, that hid the code in Elgar's music? It was something she wanted me to have one day. I didn't know what it did. I took it to mean she was giving me the key to her heart perhaps. That we had a chance of making a go of things. And she promised,' his voice wavered again, 'that when we got back to England there was something else she wanted me to have.'

'But she never made it back to England?'

Friedman shook his head.

'And Granddad only gave you the key and not the letter she'd written to explain.'

'Don't blame your granddad, Brodie. After your mother died I was no use to anybody. It wasn't my fault she died, but I believed it was. That's why, when Kerrith first told you what I'd done, I couldn't bring myself to explain. When I knew you'd heard what had happened

321

it was like I was losing your mother all over again. And this time I was losing much more. That's why, whatever happens, we have to beat these people who took the truth from us for so long; who always take the truth and bury it.'

'And you really think we can beat the Suppressors?'

'Well, you've got to admit we're doing our best to try,' he said. 'But it's not just us, Brodie. There's others. Caught in their web of deception.'

'Miss Longman and Evie and Mr Willer?'

'And many more.'

'Where do they keep them?' she asked nervously.

'Underground somewhere,' he said. 'A place of shadows where the sun never reaches.'

'Like Plato's cave?'

Friedman looked impressed. 'Perhaps.'

'So there's loads to do, then,' said Brodie. 'There's people to save and Smithies said we need to go to America and track down a ring and there's Thomas Jefferson Beale and perhaps a map.'

Friedman lifted one of his hands awkwardly from the bed and a spark of pain flashed in his eyes. 'And I've got a daughter to get to know,' he said.

Brodie helped him lower his hand. 'You know, Sir Bedivere lost a hand in battle,' she said. 'He was the first and most important Knight of Neustria.'

'You've mentioned them before,' Friedman said quizzically.

'Well, that's what we are,' she said. 'Modern Knights of Neustria.'

'And what is your quest?' he said.

'To find Avalon,' she said matter-of-factly.

'And am I a Knight of Neustria?' he asked.

Brodie waited for a moment before she answered. 'You are now,' she said.

They sat for a moment, a million words unspoken between them, but it didn't matter. The silence wasn't awkward or painful. It felt right. It felt like home.

Suddenly there was a knock on the door. 'You done with your catch-up, B?' came Hunter's voice as he pushed the door open. 'Cos I don't know if anyone else has noticed but it's actually Easter Sunday today.' He smiled broadly. 'The hotel shop has these on special offer but Smithies is insisting I can't start eating my eggs till everyone has one.' He dropped three cardboard boxes on to the foot of the bed and began to break open the lids and foil wrapping. 'Help me out, B. The wait's killing me.'

Brodie laughed and broke the chocolate egg into bite-sized pieces. She glanced across at Friedman. They'd all learnt something about the cost of waiting in the last few days. But they'd have to wait still longer for more answers. Until then though, they had each other again.

Brodie stuffed a hunk of chocolate into her mouth. 'Want some chocolate, Dad?' she said, and the man who'd fallen from the tower of light and risen again like a phoenix smiled at her and nodded.

'Thanks,' he said, and she knew he was thanking her for more than the pieces of Easter egg.

AUTHOR'S NOTE

THE TOWER OF LIGHT

When I first planned *Secret Breakers*, I knew I would write the scene involving Friedman and Brodie at the Belle Tout Lighthouse in Eastbourne. I could see it in my head from the very beginning of the series. My family and I love to take walks along the Beachy Head cliffs where the lighthouse stands. The coast is eroding year by year and in the past, Belle Tout has been moved back from the edge to stop it crashing from the cliffs and falling into the sea. I love the idea of lighthouses being guiding towers in times of trouble ... and I certainly planned for there to be a whole lot of trouble happening at Belle Tout!

A FAMOUS UNBROKEN CODE

The Shepherd's Monument at Shugborough Hall was also always going to be included in the series. Any list of famous unsolved codes is bound to mention the monument and so I knew I had to include it in my stories. While I tried to find out as much as I could about the Shepherd's Monument, I read about the other buildings and sculptures at Shugborough. I became intrigued by the Tower of the Winds and was excited I'd found another unusual building to include in the story. For me the buildings and locations become like characters and the more unusual the better!

Neither the Tower of the Winds or Belle Tout were quite as unusual as Fuller Follies though ...

FULLER'S FASCINATING FOLLIES

All the follies I describe really exist. The pyramid grave is my favourite. It is, as Hunter says, really quite incredible to see a huge stone pyramid in a tiny English churchyard.

The follies are quite close together and so it was easy to visit all of them when planning the story. The Sugarloaf was apparently built overnight in response to a bet, just as I describe in the story. Local legend suggests Fuller was totally eccentric, hence his nickname Mad Jack. His idea of having a wall built just to give people work to do, made him a fascinating character, both in life and in death!

THE POWER OF POEMS

Fuller was a great link to Belle Tout and Shugborough as he financed the building of the original lighthouse where Belle Tout is positioned and he knew the Anson family. Other exciting links in this adventure were found in poems. One of my favourite poets is Tennyson. Before I began writing the *Secret Breakers* series, I read his poem *Idylls of the King*. It sparked my interest in Arthurian legend and stories about Avalon. *The Lady of Shalott* is another beautiful Tennyson poem. I love the use of the tower in the poem and the idea of seeing the world through a mirror is a really sad but powerful one! It reminded me that in Plato's Cave Story, people don't see the world as it truly is. This is a central idea in *Secret Breakers*. And of course, using mirrors became central to solving some of the codes in the story.

THE POWER OF CODES

And congratulations to you for working out how to break this code. That is excellent secret breaking so well done. I'm very impressed!

The idea of using a mirror to break the code of the Shepherd's Monument came from the Poussin picture, Et in Arcadia Ego. The monument version is a mirror reversal and is almost identical apart from this fact and the inclusion of a pyramid. And so that was the further link to the Fuller Follies I needed.

Mirror writing is often described as a simple cipher. If you have a mirror handy then of course mirror writing is very easy to read. But mirror writing is actually very tricky to do. It is claimed that some people can do it quite naturally. One very famous mirror writer was Leonardo Da Vinci who wrote most of his private notes this way and only didn't use mirror writing when he wanted his notes to be read by other people. Now you have had a go at reading using a mirror maybe you could try writing this way too. Good luck!

WESTMINSTER ABBEY

Having decided to use Tennyson's work in this story, I thought it would be a good idea to see if his grave included any strange symbols or codes.

In this book, as in others in the series, I found that answers are often found on gravestones. Everything I describe in Westminster Abbey is really there, even the long boxes that Team Veritas hide in when they are trying to escape from Kerrith. Can you imagine how excited I was when I looked at the graves in Poets' Corner and noticed pictures of a phoenix, a griffin and some blossom? The picture that looks so much like a Tower of the Winds on Gerard Manley Hopkins' memorial stone was one of the last connectors I needed to make all the pieces of the puzzle fit together. Then I looked closely around Poets' Corner and saw the statue of Shakespeare! Its detail and location near to other statues is just as I describe and I felt I really was uncovering secrets that had been hidden for Knights of Neustria to find! The puzzle was complete!

Leicester Square in London has undergone a few changes since I first began writing this adventure and I'm not sure that the mile markers on the ground I mention are still there; but they are still important. And there are plans to return the statue of Shakespeare to the centre of the square where he stood before the renovations began and where he was when I first started planning the story. I hope people will be able to see the statue in the abbey and the statue in the square and wonder, like I did, about the changes made and what secrets they could be hiding!

A SHIP FULL OF TREASURE

As I became closer to writing the end of the *Secret Breakers* series, I began to look for connections to places further away. I was thrilled to read all about the Nuestra Señora de Covadonga, a treasure ship captured by Lord Anson. I think it was the use of the word 'nuestra' that made me stop and look twice at this part of history as I was working through my research. You have to admit that the word looks similar to Neustria and although this word is used in front of lots of ships names, seeing it used before the word Covadonga made me slow down and take notice. As always, the fun of writing *Secret Breakers* has been focusing on the tiny details. I noticed the character named Thomas Jefferson Beale had a similar name to a past US president. The 'Beale' part of his name reminded me of 'Belle' in 'Belle Tout'. And these discoveries led me to a whole new world of codes across the sea which I am excited to explore with you in the next *Secret Breakers* adventure, *The Pirate's Sword*.

To find out more check out
www.hldennis.com